"You always want to fish on the transitions,
where the ripple meets the deep."

Ripple Meets the Deep

Jason Tinney

Baltimore, Maryland

© 2014, Jason Tinney

Library of Congress Control Number: 2014947840
ISBN 978-1-936328-19-2

CityLit Project is a 501(c)(3) Nonprofit Organization
Federal Tax ID Number: 20-0639118

Printed in the United States of America, First Edition/1p
Editor and Designer: Gregg Wilhelm
Cover Design: Brian Slagle
Author Photograph: Skye Sadowski-Malcom
All characters appearing in this work are fictitious.
Any resemblance to real persons, living or dead, is purely coincidental.

CityLit Press is the imprint of nonprofit CityLit Project,
Baltimore's literary arts center.

c/o CityLit Project
120 S. Curley Street
Baltimore, MD 21224
410.274.5691
www.CityLitProject.org
info@citylitproject.org
2004-2014
Celebrating ten years serving writers and readers
in Baltimore, throughout Maryland, and across the country.

"Lily"

"Then he descended into his memory, which seemed to him endless, and up from that vertigo he succeeded in bringing forth a forgotten recollection that shone like a coin under the rain, perhaps because he never looked at it, unless in a dream...These things we know, but not those that he felt when he descended into the last shade of all."

Jorge Luis Borges

Contents

Ripple Meets the Deep

Make Me a Pallet (Down on Your Floor)

A purple surgical glove, half-full of melted ice, covers my right eye as we pull into the parking lot of the La Quinta Inn and Suites. Coy, the lap steel player, is driving. He's a good looking six-foot-two stud and has no problem with the ladies; doesn't say much and smiles a lot, hence his nickname. Come to think of it, I don't even know his real name.

"You going to be okay?" he asks.

"Yep. Thanks for the lift."

Tina, the fiddle player, missed my retina by half an inch. Her bow plowed into my eye socket in the middle of a red hot rendition of Johnny Cash's "Folsom Prison Blues." The blow knocked the harmonica right out of my mouth as I was about to break from the gate and solo on the caboose of: "Well I know I had it coming, I know I can't be free, but those people keep a-movin', and that's what tortures me."

Moments after the deal went down, a woman stood at the foot of that tiny stage at Kitty Hoynes Pub in Syracuse holding a purple surgical glove filled with ice. Swooped in like an angel. Must be a nurse; shift over, thirsty for a late night drink. Glove had to have been in her purse.

I sat out the last song. Looked pretty damn silly wandering around the bar with a purple surgical glove over my eye, looking for that woman, just to thank her, but she was gone.

Wasn't it God who made honky-tonk angels?

Derecho

I

Evan thought about soft-shell crabs as he looked west, down over the Middletown Valley. He stood on the back porch of the Victorian, coated in cream and accentuated by dark brown shutters, nestled among pines, maples, and poplars, stretching into the humid mid-June air atop Braddock Mountain.

A small, white and red pinstriped airplane dove from the heights before ascending into the wispy, cloud-speckled sky, performing stomach turning loop-de-loops that no sane pilot confined to a cockpit would ever attempt. Eleven-thirty a.m. and Evan's elderly neighbor, George, was out, as he was most Friday mornings, with his radio operated Cessna.

It was a rarity for Evan to witness George's air shows. Usually, he'd be at the South Mountain Café, the coffee house and bakery he owned on Main Street in Middletown. However, he had taken the day off. His wife's college roommate, Beth, and her husband, Neil, arrived from Scottsdale and were visiting for the weekend.

"Are you going to join us?" Hannah said, stepping out onto the porch.

"Sorry, I was just about to come in."

"Are you feeling all right?" she said, kissing his cheek.

"Yeah. Why? Do I not look all right?"

"You look fine. You're just out here alone and I was wondering—I wanted to make sure you were okay."

"I'm fine," Evan said.

"When's the doctor's appointment?"

"Monday at nine."

Hannah kissed him again. This time on the lips. "Thank you."

•

Hannah sat next to Beth and Neil, who were lounging on the couch.

"So, crab cakes this evening?" Beth said.

"That's the plan," Evan said, taking a seat in the rocker by the fireplace.

"Well, it's our treat," she said. "Years ago I was in Baltimore for a conference and we went out to a seafood restaurant at the harbor and they had these picnic tables covered with brown wrapping paper piled with all those boiled crabs."

"Steamed, dear," her husband said. "In Maryland, they steam crabs. Boiled, that's like a Louisiana thing."

"Steamed, boiled, whatever. Anyway, everyone was beating the crabs with hammers, like some crab-crushing contest. Very barbaric."

Hannah giggled.

"What?" Beth said.

"They're not hammers. They're mallets," she said.

"Jesus Christ. I'm surrounded by crab snobs. A crab cake sounds simple. No crushing," Beth said. "Evan, now tell me about this soft-shell thing you mentioned last night."

"You eat the crab whole."

"Come again?"

"For the crab to grow it has to molt—shed its hard shell so it can grow, and beneath that hard shell is a soft shell. You sauté it or fry it and you eat it."

"Eyes? All the insides?" Beth said.

"They clean them, remove the eyes and lungs, I think."

"New topic, Evan," Beth said. "I hear Amelia has a

boyfriend."

Evan shifted in his seat, crossed his leg, and rubbed his temple. "Pick another topic."

"What's the big deal? She's fourteen, what, a week away from summer vacation—going to be a sophomore in the fall? It was bound to happen sooner or later. Harmless puppy love. I was dating boys when I was in sixth grade."

"That figures," said Neil.

Beth ignored her husband's comment and glanced at Hannah, but directed her words to Evan. "I heard she came to you first and told you that a boy liked her and asked if she could go to the movies with him."

"It's true, I was slightly offended," Hannah confessed. "I thought that would be something a daughter would want to discuss with her mother first."

"Probably wanted to get the old man out of the way," Neil said.

"She didn't ask me anything," Evan said. "She said she needed to talk to me, and I knew what was coming; I could tell by her tone."

In her teenage years, Amelia had cultivated a classic coolness and grace accompanied by a confidence that pulled no punches when it came to discussions with her parents that carried some weight.

"She told me, point blank, that a boy 'liked' her and she wanted to go to the movies with him," Evan said. "What I did not see coming—for lack of imagination or denial, I suppose— was a group of teenage girls and boys standing in this living room, dressed in formal attire, posing for photographs and then vanishing into the evening, off to a spring dance."

Beth and Neil, Hannah too, could not contain their laughter.

Hannah added: "She's started having 'dot days.'"

"Dot days?" Neil said.

"It's her code," Hannah said.

"Ah," Beth whispered to her husband, "her period."

"All right." Evan stood abruptly. "I'm getting an iced tea. Anyone want anything?"

"Hey, when are we going to the café?" Neil asked.

"I figured you all could come by tomorrow for breakfast."

"How's business?" Beth said, picking up a copy of *Southern Living* from the floor.

"Great." Evan pulled a pitcher from the refrigerator. "Anyone?"

"Sweetened or unsweetened?" Beth said.

"Sweetened."

"Got anything diet?" Beth asked.

"Water," Evan said.

●

Evan lied; business was not great. The economy had not spared the independent coffee and baked goods industry. The end-of-the-year holiday bump had come and gone; 2014 began sluggishly, winter limped into spring and the doldrums of summer were rapidly approaching.

Hannah's freelance graphic design work brought in some income but projects were sporadic. Bills and debts were mounting.

Over the last month, Evan had been having nightmares so severe he'd wake up in a cold sweat that soaked through the mattress. He'd change his t-shirt and boxers at least once a night. Hannah kept finding bath towels twisted in the sheets the next morning.

Last week, the café enjoyed a welcomed evening rush. While Evan took orders, he felt a tingling sensation in his arms, as if they were falling asleep. His hands trembled. Sweat beaded on his forehead, which he wiped away with a napkin. He gave a customer an awkward smile. "Does it seem warm in here?"

The following morning, Evan made an appointment with his doctor.

Showered and changed, Evan returned to the living room to find no one in any hurry to get ready for the evening. Beth was still engrossed in *Southern Living* and Neil was watching highlights from last night's ballgames on ESPN.

Peering up from a book, Hannah said, "I don't know why you bothered ironing that shirt. It's going to be humid and it's supposed to rain." Then she looked at Beth: "He's a little OCD when it comes to ironing his clothes."

Evan didn't say anything. He went to the pantry and took a Werther's candy from a jar. When the mysterious symptoms appeared he decided to quit smoking. He went to the back porch, sucking on his treat.

A stiff breeze cut the humidity in half. Clouds, greedy gray fingers, clawed over the foothills of the Appalachian Mountains and consumed the blue sky. What followed was not a misshapen explosion of soggy guardian angels but a well defined charcoal cinderblock that erased the entire horizon; a unified army ripping through the gaps and passes that, more than one-hundred-and-fifty years ago, Robert E. Lee—George McClellan in hot pursuit—had crossed, bound for the tranquil banks of Antietam Creek.

Thunder rumbled like war drums. Branches of lightning spit like muzzle flash and the sky cracked like the lash of a whip. Wind shot through the living room, causing the pages of Beth's magazine to flip wildly as if taken hold by some apparition desperately in search of a key lime pie recipe.

Beth went to the porch, followed by Hannah and Neil. The rain fell like wrinkled linen, soaking subdivisions and farmland. Highway 40, The National Road—the highway that built America—turned into a slippery timber rattler, slithering possibly all the way to Cumberland, and six-hundred miles west to Vandalia, Illinois, and the Mississippi frontier.

The scene reminded Evan of a picture in a Bible he'd received for his first communion, thirty years ago. One of the Seven Plagues, Hail and Fire; God telling Moses to go to the Pharaoh: "I will send all my plagues upon your heart... And the Lord sent thunder and hail, and fire ran down to the earth..."

Bullied by the spray that whipped through the screens, the couples stepped back. The lights inside the house flickered. The recycling bin—its contents strewn throughout the backyard—cart-wheeled like tumbleweed. Wind chimes clanged out a mad melody. Weeping willows shook and leaves fell from the tulip poplars; they fluttered like sparrows.

"Holy shit." Neil pulled out his phone and held the device as if he were measuring barometric pressure.

"Are you filming this?" Hannah said.

"Hell yeah. We don't get weather like this in Arizona."

Hannah's phone rang. Billie Holiday's voice sang, "And stars fell on Alabama this night."

She read the text: "Amelia's school is on lock down."

"Lock down?" Evan said.

"There's a tornado warning."

As Hannah handed the phone to Evan, the storm disappeared. The sky was gray and silent.

•

Evan was on the phone with the café manager when Amelia finally walked into the house, forty-five minutes past her usual arrival time. She was unimpressed by, as she described, an "over-reaction" from the school system.

"A bit melodramatic if you ask me," she said. "They moved us all into rooms with no windows. It was just rain and wind; thunder and lightning. Big deal."

Evan took hold of Amelia and hugged her in a way that startled the teenager. "I love you. I'm glad you're home," he said.

A bit embarrassed, Amelia said, "Love you too."

Evan walked out the front door, and without looking back,

said, "I'm going to check the yard."

II

Sweat seeped through Evan's shirt as soon as he stepped outside. He felt dizzy.

George was back out with his Cessna. Evan picked up plastic milk cartons, crushed cardboard, and soda cans littering the puddled yard. He ducked, thinking the plane was making a low flying pass, but it was a pair of hummingbirds whirling through the flowers, stopping to hover and suck nectar from the gladiolas; ruby-throated, the only species of three hundred and forty in the world that traveled to Maryland, migrating in the spring from Central America and Southern Mexico.

Evan knew this because he read a *National Geographic* someone left in the café. Spanish explorers called them joyas voladoras—flying jewels; the hummingbird had a heart the size of a baby's fingernail and, in flight, it beat up to twelve-thousand times per minute, whereas the human heart only beat seventy times per minute.

Images of hummingbirds and Civil War generals, migration west, biblical passages, daughters dancing with boys—they were finger snaps in his head, coming faster and faster, one after the other.

Evan went inside and straight for the bedroom. The finger snaps pounded. The tingling sensation returned to his arms, but now it felt like a thousand pricking needles. He shook, his neck tightened; his body was running away.

There was a moment of clarity when he realized the possibility that this was a heart attack.

Hannah came into the bedroom and went to her jewelry box for earrings and a bracelet.

"Everything all right outside?" she said.

"I don't feel well," Evan said, struggling to push the words out of his mouth. "I need help."

Hannah turned to see her husband laying on the bed, trembling, clammy, his face white as the shirt he was wearing. "I'm taking you to the doctor right now and we're going to find out what the hell is going on."

"I need to go to the emergency room."

"All right, just try to relax," Hannah said. "I'm going to tell everyone what the situation is and I will take you."

"Call an ambulance. I think I'm having a heart attack."

Hannah processed the words. She calmly walked to the phone on the nightstand and dialed 911.

Evan tried to form words but nothing came out of his mouth. He looked down and saw his hand scraping away at his chest. He couldn't find his heart.

Hannah put down the phone and sat down next to him on the bed. He couldn't hear her. All he knew was the words she spoke were comforting; he felt the vibration of her voice and her touch and held onto them like falling feathers. Sweat mixed with tears and burned his eyes.

Evan reached out to Hannah. He wanted to climb inside her heart, which had always been a safe place to hide.

She took hold of his hand and all Evan could force out of his mouth was: "Help me, help me."

III

"I think I'm going to throw up." Evan pulled the oxygen mask from his mouth.

Another round of showers began as a middle-aged, pudgy paramedic with black, Buddy Holly-style spectacles, walkie-talkie at his hip attached to a leather strap hanging around his shoulder, wheeled Evan into the emergency room.

"Hey, Evan," the paramedic said, "do me a favor. Don't throw up on me. We've come too far for that."

"Okay."

"Hey partner," the paramedic said, placing the mask back over Evan's mouth, "do you smoke?"

"I quit last week."

"That's amazing. You've got great lung capacity."

"I swim."

"Great cardio exercise. You want some more good news?"

"Sure," Evan said.

"I don't think you're having a heart attack."

•

Hannah arrived and was taken to the exam room where a beautiful Hispanic woman was returning with Evan's urine results and more compliments.

"It looks just gorgeous," the nurse said, picking up a chart.

The doctor examined the EKG, studying the spikes and dips of ink and confirmed the paramedic's assertion. Evan was not having a heart attack but a severe panic attack.

"A panic attack?" Hannah said.

The symptoms often mirror those of a heart attack, the doctor explained.

"Sometimes these 'panics' just come out of the blue. I want you to follow up with your primary care physician," he said, jotting notes on Evan's chart.

"He has an appointment Monday morning," Hannah said.

"Good. I'll send the info over to their office. But before I can let him go we have to get that blood pressure down."

Evan's BP was clocking in at an alarming one seventy-eight over ninety-two, but he wasn't paying attention to the doctor's words. He was focused on the IV that the nurse was preparing to put into his arm.

"I have to tell you something," Evan said, urgency rising with each word. "I'm really bad with needles."

"Don't worry, baby," she said with a soft smile and a wink. "I'm really good with them."

Evan closed his eyes and turned away.

The doctor had prescribed a small dose of Ativan. Evan couldn't watch the liquid drip into his vein.

"Honey?"

He opened his eyes. Hannah was sitting next him, moving her hand across his damp hair.

"You need to take deep breaths," she said. "Everything is going to be fine. Put a calm picture in your mind. We'll be out of here soon."

The hummingbirds came into his head, but he didn't want to think about their heartbeats. Then everything slowed and he saw not darting, frantic animals but majestic, sugar-sucking "flying jewels" and he marveled at a fact he'd forgotten: The heart of a hummingbird makes up two-and-a-half percent of its total body weight, making it, proportionally, the largest heart in the world.

"Where's Amelia?" Evan asked.

"She's fine. She's home with Beth and Neil. They're going to order a pizza and watch a movie."

"Okay," Evan said. "Can you let her know that I'm fine?"

"Yes," Hannah said. "I'm going to make some phone calls. Are you going to be all right if I leave you alone for a bit?"

"Of course."

"Will you be offended if I walk across the street to get a coffee at Starbucks?" she asked.

"No," Evan said. "I sometimes go to Starbucks."

•

"We are doing a brisk business tonight," the nurse said, wheeling another patient into Evan's exam room. "I've got a two-for-one deal. Evan, meet Alex. You two are going to be roommates till another room opens up."

The nurse left. Alex, a young, slender man, looked over at Evan. "So, what brings you in on this lovely evening?" he asked.

"I thought I was having a heart attack, but it turned out to be a panic attack," Evan mumbled, embarrassed, as if a panic attack did not warrant ambulances and emergency rooms.

"Panic attack. Are you in finance?"

"Not exactly," Evan said. "I own a coffee shop and bakery."

"Small business," Alex said. "I'd be having a panic attack, too. I work for a military contractor. We're not going out of business anytime soon."

Evan, annoyed at the comment, shifted in his bed, trying not to disturb his IV. Establishing his territory, he turned on the television.

"What's your story?" Evan said, watching the local news.

"Not sure yet. I've got this pain that comes and goes down here on my right," Alex said, pointing to an area just below his abdomen. "At first, I thought it might be my hernia. Had an operation when I was a teenager. They plugged it up with a metal mesh. But they say it's not a hernia."

"It might be a kidney stone," Evan suggested, warmer now, turning to Alex. "Or your appendix. Isn't the appendix on the right side?"

"That's what they're testing for now. No one mentioned kidney stones. Shit, that's going to make pissing fun."

Returning to the TV, Evan said, "I'm sure it will work out fine."

A news reporter, in heavy-duty storm gear, stood in front of a car, its hood and windshield crushed from an oak split in two. Other footage—images of downed power lines and a trampoline, apparently lifted by strong winds, or a tornado, that had come to rest on the roof of a house—flashed across the screen.

"It's a derecho," Alex said.

"A derecho?"

"Yeah, it's like this massive storm that just bitch-slapped a third of the country. Cut a thousand mile path from the Mid-West to the Mid-Atlantic."

"Incredible," Evan said.

"O.J.," Alex said.

"What's that?"

"O.J. Simpson. That's how I remember the hernia

operation," he said. "I was laid up for a week and the only thing on TV was the O.J. trial. I was on this heavy duty Tylenol/codeine cocktail for the pain. I tried to read, but all the words ran together, so the only thing I could do was watch television and every channel was showing the O.J. trial, replays of the white Bronco low-speed chase, images of Nicole Simpson and the bloody glove."

"God," Evan said. "O.J. When was that, '92?"

"Ninety-five. Murder happened in '94 and trial began in January, '95."

Evan finally looked at his IV and the liquid dripping into his arm. "Didn't something happen in '92?"

"The L.A. riots."

"That's right," Evan said. The Ativan was working and he suddenly felt social. "My wife's college roommate is visiting for the weekend. They went to the University of Southern California. She visited the campus her senior year of high school. She and her folks flew three-thousand miles and landed on the first day of the riots; she watched the whole thing unfold from a hotel window."

"That's something else," Alex said. "When the O.J. thing was happening I was thirteen and having this affair."

The nurse walked into the exam room. "How are my two favorite boys doing?"

"We're doing okay," Alex said. "Any results on my tests?"

"Not yet, soon."

The nurse checked Evan's blood pressure. "Now that's what I like to see. It's coming down, baby."

When the nurse left, Evan said: "You were having an affair when you were thirteen? What are you talking about?"

"When I was thirteen, my first was with a forty-five-year-old married woman," Alex said. "I mowed her lawn. One day, she asked me if I wanted a sandwich. I said yes, and she invited me in. I ate the sandwich, and she gave me a Coke. She smiled; I finished the Coke. I was so sweaty from mowing she asked if I wanted to take a shower. I said, 'I don't know.' Then she told me to go upstairs and take a shower and I did. After that, I took a shower every day I mowed her lawn, and she took a shower with me. That was the beginning."

"The beginning of what?" Evan said.

"My string of disasters with women," Alex said. "I got the hernia and she left her husband and moved to Fort Wayne, Indiana. She never said goodbye or anything like that. Just moved. She destroyed me."

Stumbling for some kind of response, Evan said, "Well, uh, those are pretty extreme circumstances. You were thirteen, she was an older woman. She seduced you. I mean, that's got to leave, I don't know, an impression?"

"Maybe," Alex said, rubbing his side. "I've never been with another woman who made me feel the way she made me feel. I still see those soapy breasts now and then, and remember drying off in her bedroom. It's a kind of beautiful pain that digs down in your bones. You ever felt anything like that?"

Evan remembered that forty-five minutes before meeting this man, he was lying in his bed clinging to the rhythm of his wife's voice and her heart. Then he remembered the day she walked into his café looking for fresh baked Irish soda bread, and since it was March, he did indeed have fresh baked Irish soda bread. Hannah bought two loaves. She returned the next day and purchased another loaf not mentioning the quality of the loaves she had bought previously.

Evan did not see a ring and completely bypassed an inquiry about a boyfriend and simply asked, "Would you like to have dinner sometime?" He'd never been that forward with a woman. Strange how Irish soda bread could catapult two people into a life together.

"Yes," Evan said.

"Good," Alex said. "A man shouldn't go through life without experiencing that once."

The nurse entered the exam room. "Alex, the doctor is coming to speak with you. You may be staying with us a little while longer," she said. "And Evan, you're going home."

The nurse wheeled Evan out and Alex stopped her. "Evan, it was good talking to you. Don't worry so much."

●

Discharged, Evan and Hannah walked across the parking lot to their car. The rain had stopped and steam rose from the asphalt.

Evan took a long, deep breath and exhaled and prepared for what was about to come next.

Make Me a Pallet
(Move It On Over)

I don't do the things I used to do because I'm not allowed. I've made a pact with my girlfriend. Sophia has joined me on this short tour of upstate New York. Her recent knee injury requires a swimming pool for daily exercise, which the La Quinta has and the Microtel, just up the road where the rest of the band is staying, does not.

This is the story we are sticking by.

Truth be told, Sophia is keeping an eye on me due to my "condition," as she calls it. My condition is not yet clinically defined; however, I've diagnosed the ailment as not knowing what to do with myself. The current treatment: Do nothing and refrain from kicking holes in walls.

About six months ago, not knowing what to do with myself led to abusive behavior toward various household items. One evening after a heated argument I mistook the vacuum cleaner for a sledgehammer and drilled it into the hardwood floor, shattering the Electrolux to bits. In another melodramatic display, I put my fist through the bathroom mirror. When Sophia came home she calmly stated, "Well, that's a lovely spider web of rage."

Too much, too many—too much booze and too many late nights and encounters with ex-girlfriends, where nostalgia led me by the hand to the edge of dangerous cliffs. The culmination: I returned home drunk after a gig and fell into our metal hammock stand. The bleeding gash in the middle of my forehead required eleven stitches.

Sophia told me that we needed to have a come-to-Jesus

meeting. Chill out. Wise up. Or get out.

I had become a calamity.

The Mouth of Possibility

Her eyes came to him softly that morning. Alone on the beach, Lada rubbed her finger across his chin, the stubble reminding her of autumn's first frost. They were miles from any roads; so far north along the Carolina Outer Banks that the Virginia state line could be seen, marked by a broken fence half-buried in the dune. It made her feel good to be away from roads.

"Roads," she said, "somehow reassure people they are connected to civilization. Take away roads and something primal bubbles to the surface, impulses, a subconscious tie to a time when there was very little clothing. Erotic, actually, in an instinctual sort of way."

The ocean, endless and sprawling, the moon's tug of the tide slipping into the horizon, "the mouth of possibility," Lada said, her delicate Eastern European accent framing her words no longer chained to teenage years when sirens called out a rusted moan and bombs fell on Karlovac, while she and her family took shelter in the bathroom, the safest place in their home. Origins were no longer her concern; she was bathed in the liberation of the present.

Lada met Andrew the day before at a flea market in Duck. All she knew was that he had an online antiques store called We Got Permission, a site that specialized in junk, as he called it: vintage oyster cans, old railroad glass power line insulators, luggage from the 1940s, vinyl records and such. He told her he was born in Accident, Maryland. She didn't believe him.

"Yes," Andrew said, "it's in the mountains of Western Maryland, just about as far west as you can go before you cross into the Heartland of America."

Lada didn't argue. She knew nothing about the state of Maryland. The less she knew the better. After the encounter was over she'd return to Tampa and never see him again.

They didn't talk much anyway, resolved that words and action rarely coincided in harmony. However, he did find amusement in Americanisms she still hadn't quite grasped but nonetheless attempted to work into conversation: take the bull by the hooves; the shit's going to hit the fence; cut me some slacks.

It was balmy—unseasonably warm for late November. As they walked barefoot along the beach, Andrew touched the back of her head. A cropped cut exposed a long, slender neck. Her hair—the color of honey—was divided down the middle and two long wisps dripped down on her pale cheeks.

When they came to the dead shark that had washed up on the beach, she put her hand to her mouth. It was maybe seven-feet long, nibbled, the last ounce of dignity stolen when someone came along and jammed a two-by-four down its throat.

"That's just awful," Lada said. "Who the hell would do such a thing?"

She knelt down and put her hands around the two-by-four. When she pulled, Andrew felt her hands move inside of him and tasted the sand in her mouth on his tongue as the wood scraped against cartilage, moving through the shark's stomach, past the cold, silent heart.

She stood and tossed the two-by-four aside. She tilted her head, slipping a dangling strand of hair behind an ear and examined the fish as if it were a sculpture in the midst of creation. Lada got down on her knees and carefully reached into the shark's mouth, navigating rows of razor teeth until she came to the tooth she wanted.

She wiggled the tooth free and held it in her hand and marched into the lapping foam and water singing: "Their old rusty rapiers that hung by their sides, we flung them as far as we could in the tide…Now take them up devils!"

With all her strength, she threw the tooth into the broad Atlantic, into the mouth of all that possibility.

Make Me a Pallet (Wayfaring Stranger)

I ditch the surgical glove and walk through the sliding doors with an amp and a fishing tackle box full of Hohner harmonicas. It's after 2 a.m.

I nod to the desk clerk and head to the lobby lounge, taking a seat in a well-cushioned sofa in front of a flat screen television. The LPGA is on; lady golfers are getting pretty sexy.

The desk clerk mutters to the security guard, "Creepy drunks coming home." The La Quinta is across the road from Turning Stone, an Indian casino/resort owned by the Oneida Nation, the same tribe calling for the Washington Redskins to change their name.

"Full moon," says the security guard.

The group entering the lobby doesn't look drunk at all, on the contrary, quite lucid and lively despite flesh falling from their faces; exposed, disease-ridden cheek tendons; holes in chests where still-beating hearts hang from arteries; missing limbs, bloody stumps of bone; and a tall man pulling a Samsonite suitcase and carrying a chainsaw, wearing a mismatched tweed suit and a mask that appears to be sewn together out of dried, human skin.

SCARE-A-CON, "the northeast's premiere horror and sci-fi convention," is being held at the casino. I read about it in a brochure. Linda Blair, the actress who made vomiting pea soup an art form, is the headliner.

The guard and clerk don't bat an eye as the attendees head for the elevator. Instead, they stare at me.

I get it: threadbare jeans, beat-up cowboy boots with Gorilla tape across one heel; filthy Fender amp, tackle box and no fishing gear. I'm reminded of the joke about the musician trying to get into heaven and Saint Peter tells him to go around to the back and don't touch any of the food as he loads his gear through the kitchen.

I'm put at ease, if for no other reason than normalcy, when two prostitutes walk through the lobby clinging to the arms of two clean-cut men in their 60s. Decked out in tailored suits, they haven't bothered to take off their wedding rings and, really, why does it matter? It is what it is. For everyone involved, it's just business.

Salt Refused

It is the week before Halloween and Lucy, in her late 30s, has left her home in Baltimore and returned to live with her mother, Alice—late 50s—in Cambridge on the Eastern Shore of Maryland. She stands with a large suitcase in the living room, which looks like a scene from the reality show, Hoarders. *The room is decorated in a half-assed fashion for Halloween and a full box of decorations lies on the floor next to the couch. Sweaters, producing a pungent smell of mothballs, are stuffed into a plastic milk crate on a rocking chair by the front window. An old-fashioned ice-cream maker sits at the foot of the stairs leading to the bedrooms. Dozens of DVDs and VHS cassettes are strewn around the television. Leaning against the wall are three ugly oil paintings of a skipjack, a blue crab, and a rockfish; a Post-It on the portrait of the crab reads: Eastern Shore Icons. The side of the living room, closest to the kitchen, doubles as the dining room. On an oval table, atop newspaper, sits a large pumpkin. In a corner stand three stationary bicycles.*

Lucy takes her luggage upstairs. Her mother enters the front door with several plastic grocery bags and goes to the kitchen. Lucy returns to the living room with a Strawberry Shortcake cereal bowl full of acorns. She pushes a pile of various catalogs aside and sits on the couch, placing the bowl on the coffee table. She gives the living room another look, lights a cigarette, and speaks:

What is this shit?

Alice enters the living room drinking a can of Coors Light. She holds a wooden spoon and a large knife.

When'd you get here?

Just a few minutes ago. Getting ready for a yard sale?

No, why?

Just wondering. Mom, what are these?

Those are acorns.

I know they're acorns. I found them upstairs in my closet. I'm just curious—why are there acorns in my closet?

Squirrels, I think.

Squirrels?

I think they're living in the closet and storing acorns for the winter.

There are squirrels living in the closet?

I think so. There's a hole in the roof. I think that's how they're getting in.

Have you seen them?

No. I'm afraid to go in there. Back over the summer, I went looking for a box of old 45s and saw all those acorns. I meant to warn you but you beat me to the punch.

And the cereal bowl?

Well, the acorns were scattered everywhere. I wanted to collect them in one place so the squirrels would know where to put their food.

Alice takes a swig of her beer, stabs the top of the pumpkin, horror-movie style. Lucy stubs out her cigarette.

Mom, think we should talk?

If I don't tell you this now I'll forget. I had the strangest morning. I'm on my way to the Food Lion. I'm at a traffic light by the Wawa. This car pulls up behind me. I look in the rearview mirror. It's a mother, a father, and two teenage boys in the back seat. When the car comes to a complete stop, all four of them duck down. For some reason, I thought they were putting on ski masks and they were going to carjack me. Those kinds of things are happening all the time. The crime around Cambridge—it's just terrible.

Before you go any further with this story, I'm going to assume you were not carjacked.

No, I was not carjacked—just let the story come to you. When the family reappears, they all have boxes of Popeye's fried chicken and they're devouring the chicken like a pack of wild dogs. I get to the Food Lion; get my groceries and I'm at the register and there's a man behind me and he has seventeen bottles of yellow mustard—store brand. I don't know why I said this, it just came out of my mouth. I smiled at the man and said, "Like mustard?" He looked at me as if I was crazy.

Don't know why he'd think that.

Well, I'm in the parking lot and realize it's a sign.

A sign? Let me guess. Four passengers in a car, four boxes of fried chicken; four times four is sixteen and there were seventeen bottles of mustard: 4-4-16-17. Those are the lotto numbers you played?

Bingo! That's my girl.

Alice takes another sip of beer.

All right, girl, let's get into this. You told me over the phone. 'Course, had to hear most of the story from your Aunt Mary first, but that's beside the point. So, what happened up there in the city?

Lucy slaps her thighs and stands; circles around the couch and picks through the box of Halloween decorations.

Couldn't stop.

Alice continues to carve the pumpkin. She says nothing.

Plane crashed into the side of the mountain. Opened full throttle and pulled a Casey Jones. Every cliché, that's me. Drunk. Rock bottom. Lost my kids, my home, my husband— well, Paul was going to leave me anyway.

Another woman?

Who? Him or me?

You started sleeping with a woman?

No. Thought about it though. Thought about sleeping with other men. Paul may have been seeing someone. I wouldn't know.

Lucy stops picking through the decorations and moves to her mother.

Mom, I want you to know something. I never put those

kids in harm's way. I was never passed out when they got...

"Functioning drunk." That's what they're called, right?

Yes, "functioning drunk." Functioning fuck-up. I don't know.

Of course you do. Everyone knows what they are. Don't know—horseshit. And don't give me any therapy babble about unhappiness. Happiness is something they made up, like Valentine's Day.

Sage advice has always been your forté.

Don't walk in here passing judgment on me.

I'm not judging you. But, I'm going to ask a favor. Please don't drink in front of me.

Alice slams the knife down on the table, takes her beer, and walks into the kitchen. She grabs a travel coffee mug from a cabinet. The mug has a red crab on it and reads: "Don't bother me, I'm crabby." She pours the beer into the mug and walks back into the dining room, resuming her carving.

Happy now? How would you feel if I said I don't like you smoking in my house?

There's an ashtray here on the coffee table.

Maybe it's not for cigarettes.

What's it for? Collecting acorns?

Maybe it's for paperclips. What you need to do is dry out and get your head straight. Prohibition ain't coming back just because you can't handle your booze.

Lucy returns to the couch; resumes her story.

I wrecked the car and went to jail. Have a court date coming up. Paul filed for divorce, which I signed off on as well as the arrangement where he would have custody with supervised visits, to be revisited once I get my shit straightened out. I did the inpatient rehab, A.A., got the interlock on the car, etcetera, etcetera.

Alice stops carving. Looks down at the table and takes a sip from the mug.

When's the last time you saw the kids?

A few weeks ago, before I came down here. Had breakfast at a Denny's—Moons Over My Hammies all around. Paul sat at the counter drinking coffee, reading the paper.

I know this must be killing you.

It's not killing me. I destroyed everything. It's strange, but I feel hope. There's nothing left to lose. I feel like slackwater.

That moment when the tides change and the water is perfectly still.

Alice rips off the top of the pumpkin, seeds clinging to the stringy insides. She digs in with the wooden spoon and slops the guts onto the newspaper. Alice points the spoon at Lucy.

Well, just don't come into my house and judge me. I didn't refuse you. I said you could come home—giving you shelter in your time of need. I've been refused plenty of times when I needed a place to stay.

Mom, I'm not judging you.

Yes you are—yard sale, what's that supposed to mean? Since the day you learned the meaning of the word judgment you've been judging me. Guess you blame me for the mess you're in.

I just got through telling you that everything that's happened is my fault.

Lucy lights another cigarette.

Lucy, you know what your problem is?

Enlighten me.

Do you know where you were when you got engaged?

This has to do with my problem?

Do you know where you were when you got engaged, where Paul proposed to you?

Fort McHenry.

Do you know where I was?

You were here.

I was here, and do you remember what I said to you when you called with the news?

Congratulations.

So was I not supportive—dare I say happy for you, Lucy?

You could have been saying congratulations to a complete stranger at a gas station.

But I didn't say congratulations to a complete stranger, I said it to you.

Is there a point?

Yes, there's a point. Do you remember what I was doing when you called?

I have no clue.

I was in bed watching *Blue Hawaii*. It was the scene where Elvis—as Chadwick Gates—is floating down the lagoon in that canoe with all those tropical flowers. Well, I saw that movie with your father when we were dating and during that very scene, in that dark movie theater, he put his arm around me and kissed me and I knew right then and there that we were going to be married and have a long life together.

Put your money on the wrong horse.

That's the goddamn point exactly, Lucy. Just another fucking horse race. We all got bamboozled by Elvis Presley and Blue Hawaii!

I'm not following you.

You should have known better. You thought Chadwick Gates was going to save you.

I've never seen *Blue*-fucking-*Hawaii*.

You saw what happened to me and your father. You want your kids to see your mistakes. That's the only real lesson you can teach them. You want your kids to make their own mistakes—not yours.

Well, I'm doing a dynamite job in that department.

Lucy, there is no such thing as Chadwick Gates. There never was an Elvis Presley. It's all made up.

Make Me a Pallet
(She Gave Me Gasoline)

The security guard strolls into the lounge and gives me a polite, non-threatening smile. I keep watching ladies golf. A magnificent Asian beauty nails a twenty-two-foot putt.

"Sir, are you staying here?" he says.

I slowly take my eyes from the screen. "Yes, I am."

"What room, sir?"

"Two-thirteen." I immediately realize that the number doesn't sound right. "Sorry, two-twenty-three."

He gives me a hard once-over. "Okay, sir, you have yourself a good morning."

Feeling I've overstayed my welcome, I take the elevator to the second floor. The green light flashes when I slide the card key. The bathroom light is on, and I brush my teeth and climb into bed. Sophia turns on her side. I kiss the back of her neck.

I haven't bothered to undress and not five minutes goes by before I'm out the door, creeping down the hallway, hip flask of Wild Turkey in my pocket, listening for mischief, puking, giggling, groaning, screaming. With SCARE-A-CON in town somebody could be slashed to death and no one would notice.

That's why I can't sleep in hotels. There's always something happening and I don't want to miss a thing.

Out in the parking lot, a slight breeze has cooled the early morning darkness. I take a sip from the flask and go wandering.

Smoking a cigarette, I scan license plates. I see our Jeep with its Maryland plates and others: New York and New Jersey, of course, and there's Wisconsin, Ontario, Ohio, New Mexico, Pennsylvania, Georgia.

I bought the Jeep new four years ago and have clocked more than one-hundred-thousand miles. There's a piece of black tape over the odometer. Miles no longer matter. It's useless to get sentimental over oil-stained asphalt. Like birthdays, all those brief moments worn down to the rubber.

A crowd of smokers is loitering, the last of the last-call refugees from the neighboring sports bar with the unfortunate name, Recovery. The security guard and a shuttle bus driver from the casino are having a conversation on the sidewalk.

Someone is screaming by a dumpster, out of sight, toward the rear of the hotel. It's a female voice, her large shadow cast by a spotlight above the side entrance. Finally, she appears spitting vitriol into her cell phone: "We broke up two weeks ago, motherfucker. What you don't seem to understand is how much I hate you. I hate the way you dress, the way you tie your shoes. I hate the way you eat your food, the way you swallow your food. I fucking hate the way you breathe."

She hangs up and returns to the crowd. "Christ," she says. "I'm so fucking sick of hearing his face."

She lights a cigarette and takes a deep drag, cocks her head back and pumps out smoke.

"Christ, give me a fucking break," she says. "Yesterday morning, I heard my ten-year-old son call his younger sister a bitch. I grabbed him by his collar and said, 'Don't you ever call your sister a bitch again. Don't ever call any woman a bitch. I hear that word come out of your mouth one more time, you're going to have a daily diet of soap.'"

Taking another long drag, she says, "Only problem is his sister is a bitch."

Approaching the guard and driver, I say, "'Sick of hearing his face,' that's a new one. Must be that full moon."

The guard watches the woman get into her car. "No, she's always like that. She works over at Recovery."

"She's a regular there, too," says the driver, typing something into his iPhone. "Never shit where you eat."

Luck of the Glove

Across the street from the treatment center he visited once a week to confront an inability to stay out of his own way, Harry retraced his steps through Maryvale Park looking for his black, leather gloves. He had come into the gloves under slightly dubious circumstances and knew he was bound to lose them sooner or later. Harry was certain someone had picked them up. His only wish: that whoever had the gloves, they get as much use out of them as he had over the last five years.

He discovered the gloves in the parking lot of a resort in the mountains of southern Virginia where he and his wife were honeymooning. They looked expensive. Most likely, they'd fallen out of a pocket or car door while someone was loading or unloading their luggage.

His wife noticed the gloves right away when he returned to their room. Feeling no need to lie, Harry told her how he'd come across them. She said they were nice and someone must miss them, shouldn't he take them to the front desk to be placed in the lost and found?

By the time he'd reached the lobby, Harry had concocted a plan to get the gloves back. He'd give it twenty-four hours.

The following morning, he inquired if anyone had turned in a pair of soft, black leather gloves. The woman, a warm Southern belle with a rich Virginia accent, produced the gloves and placed them on the counter.

"Looking for these?" she asked.

"I sure am," he said with an appreciative smile. "Thank

you so much."

•

Harry's futile searching turned to aimless strolling. Maryvale was part of a neighborhood called Brigadoon, named after the musical starring Gene Kelly. Developed in the 1950s, the red and white ranchers, built upon curving, tree-shaded streets were billed as a "magical place to live," not far from where construction had begun on US Route 15. West of the highway that connected Rebel Virginia to Yankee Pennsylvania, vibrant farmland waited for evaporation into the Golden Mile, four lanes of asphalt distended with strip malls and fast food joints.

Harry stopped at the storm drain where, nearly thirty years ago, he and his cousin, Ben, would sneak smokes. The tunnel, essentially a sewage pipe, was large enough to ride a dirt bike through.

The summer before their freshman year of high school, Harry and Ben bought their first pack of Marlboro Reds from a vending machine in the foyer of the China Garden. Not that it mattered. The owners didn't give a shit if two underage boys, practically twins—identical short shocks of red hair, light freckles across the bridge of their noses—were dropping their cash on a pack. Harry and Ben probably could have gone to the take-out counter, bought their Marlboros and ordered steamed dumplings, and shrimp-fried rice.

A chain link fence separated Maryvale from the China Garden's parking lot. One afternoon, having purchased their cigarettes, Harry and Ben walked through the park to the drain. They puffed away, and Ben noticed something in the middle of the pipe. They took a closer look and discovered a stack of damp, porn magazines: *Playboy*, *Hustler*, and a few the boys had never seen before. The pages of the unfamiliar publications contained photographs of sexual acts that Harry and Ben didn't know the body could do, or body really should do.

"Holy shit, look at this," Ben said, handing a magazine to Harry.

"I don't know about you, but I wouldn't put mine in there," Harry said, pulling hard on the Marlboro. "Want to take them?"

"They belong to somebody," Ben said. "They weren't thrown away in here. They're stacked."

Ben flipped through a couple more magazines and said, "They're in alphabetical order."

"That's crazy," Harry said. "If you're smart enough to catalogue them, why are you dumb enough to hide them in a sewage drain?"

"Look."

Ben was right, they were in alphabetical order.

"That's weird shit," Harry said.

"Maybe some pervert brings kids down here and molests them," Ben said, looking at both ends of the tunnel.

Harry dropped the magazine and crushed out his cigarette. "I don't know what the hell we're doing picking up porn magazines left in a sewer—giving me the creeps. I'm getting out of here. You want to come over?"

Ben stared down at the magazines. "No. I'm going home."

•

A few days passed and they went back to the storm drain. The magazines were gone.

"Guess the perv collected his magazines," Harry said.

"I have them," Ben said, lighting a cigarette. "After we left the other day, I came back and took them home. I have them hidden in the garage."

"What the hell did you do that for?"

"I don't know," Ben said.

"We found them together. You should have consulted me."

Maybe it was the word "consulted" that triggered Ben's response. He pulled back and punched Harry square in the face, breaking his nose.

Ben didn't say a word; he just walked away, leaving Harry standing there, stunned, blood pouring from his nostrils, tears streaming down his face, holding a pack of Marlboros.

•

Harry went home that afternoon and told his parents he'd fallen off his bike riding down a hill. There was only the thinnest shred of plausibility to the story, but they accepted it and Harry's mother took him to the hospital.

Harry and Ben stopped smoking in the storm drain and never talked about the incident or the porn magazines again.

In his senior year, Ben had a falling out with his parents when, unbeknownst to them, he married a woman from El Salvador. Upon graduation, they moved to Galveston where Ben got a job with a seafood company.

Harry never saw or heard from Ben again—no one did. It's a hell of a thing severing all ties with your family.

Maybe it was some deep fear neither of them could wrap their minds around—not smoking or porn magazines—but fear rooted in a landscape shifting too fast that caused Ben to punch Harry.

Harry never found the gloves.

They never should have touched the things that didn't belong to them. They never should have started smoking.

Make Me a Pallet
(Long Distance Call)

I brush my teeth again and step into the room. From the darkness, I hear Sophia.

"You all right?" she asks.

Sitting on the bed, I pull off my boots and unsnap my Western shirt. "Yep."

"It's three in the morning," Sophia says, switching on the lamp above the nightstand.

I give her a kiss, my Saint Christopher medal hanging between us. "I couldn't sleep. I went downstairs for a smoke and watched some TV."

"What happened to your eye? It's bruised."

"Tina accidentally poked me with her bow during the show."

Sophia has never completely trusted my professional relationship with Tina and, perhaps, with good reason since there is nothing sexier than an attractive woman playing the fiddle.

"I know you were watching TV and smoking." Her head nods to the phone. "Got a call."

"A call," I say. "From who?"

"Front desk, asking me if there was a man staying in my room. The guy says, 'There was a man in the lobby who said he was staying in room 223.' And I say, 'Yes, my husband is with me.'"

"Husband?" I say.

I unbuckle my belt and pull off my jeans and shirt and toss them on a chair, and throw the socks in a corner with other dirty laundry.

"We're in our thirties; we've been living together for two

years and we're too old to call each other boyfriend and girl-friend," she says. "Partner doesn't sound right; that's what gay couples call each other."

"Not anymore. They can call each other husbands and wives."

Sophia ignores my statement, reaches for a bottle of water and continues: "I thought you were in the bathroom, but I check the bathroom—you're not there. So, I tell the guy that you must have gone to the car for something and say that I will call you on your cell phone. Then he says he has your cell phone. Found it on the couch."

I get into bed and bring the covers close to my face.

"You know what else? He says, 'Well, he's been coming and going a lot.'"

"What did you say to that?" I ask, closing my eyes.

"I said, 'Yeah, that sounds like my husband.'"

Cub Cadet

The lawn mower gleamed, yellow paint taking on a golden sheen in the afternoon sun; a 173cc Honda engine mounted on a twenty-one inch, three-in-one steel deck—"engineered for superior mulching, bagging, and side discharging." Ryan sat Indian-style examining the four knobby tires, front two on casters allowing access to the nooks and crannies of the flower beds, the maple and oak trees, the magnolia and holly bushes.

He was drawn to the mower. Cub Cadet, he whispered the words over and over again.

The mower was the last birthday gift from his wife before the separation, before she ran off to Richmond to "rediscover" herself five months ago. She bought it at H.B. Duvall, out by the fairgrounds, and paid for the extended warranty. The lawn mower sat in the garage untouched. The grass grew tall. The violet blooms and Morning Glories twisted through the tomato plants.

Ryan slid the choke back and the engine turned over on the first pull of the cord. It sounded wonderful.

He made short order of the front yard and mowed along the sides of the white Cape Cod, the house where he grew up, on the cusp of Baker Park. He plowed through the terraced back yard, cutting through thick grass like a sharp knife slicing into a watermelon.

Sweat rolled through his red hair and drained down his forehead; the salty water swimming in his eyes filled Ryan with the satisfaction that he was reclaiming domain over his yard. His footsteps were firm and even, assured inside the snuggly laced, grass-stained work boots that followed a trail blazed by self-propelled tire marks.

As he made his last pass by the garage, Ryan felt a burning pierce in his neck and instinctively smacked at the source of heat. He saw a flash of yellow zip past his eyes and then another. For a brief moment he thought he was seeing spots brought on by the warm afternoon. The thunderous humming drowned out the purr of the Cub Cadet, and he realized the full scope of his predicament. Ryan looked down and saw a hole, the size of a softball, erupting with yellow jackets. They engulfed him in a cyclone. They bore into his skin, working their stingers as if Ryan was a mad sewing project.

Struggling to remove his jeans, caught up at his boots, he fell to the ground slashing at the denim with a pocket-knife till they finally came apart at the ankles. He wrestled free from his t-shirt and ran to the house wearing only blue boxer shorts and work boots.

Welts on his body swelled. Mixing water and baking soda, he tried to get his breathing under control. The paste applied to the wounds, Ryan lay down on the cool tile.

•

Last summer, Denise's parents threw a pool party at their home and Ryan knew. She wore a new bikini. She hadn't worn a bikini in years, not since before they were married. There was no mention of this new bikini—not that one needed to be made, but Denise could have said something like, "What do you think?" or "How do I look?" And, she had started to work out.

But it wasn't the bikini, or her newly sculptured body that unnerved him as much as it was the way he felt when he looked at her—a feeling of talons reaching down into his stomach and clawing at his guts.

Standing on the deck, sipping a Coke, Ryan looked across the pool at his wife. She lay there, oil glistening on her flat-frying-pan stomach, her skin turning bronze, her eyes shaded by black wrap-around sunglasses.

Her mother brought out fruit salad while neighbors, grasping cocktail glasses in the shape of pineapples, walked in and out of the air conditioned kitchen leaving the sliding door open. Denise's father and her brother talked aimlessly about Terps football and Maryland's dismal chances of competing in the Big 10. Bits of poorly packed hamburgers fell through the grill grate disappearing into blue flames.

Denise simply lay there, oblivious, baking in the sun a million miles away.

When they got home that evening, Denise told Ryan she wanted to go for a walk around Culler Lake—by herself.

When she returned, he said, "You looked beautiful in that bikini."

"Thank you," she said, in a voice that a stranger might acknowledge a compliment from another stranger.

•

The evening was perfect for sitting outside. Recovering in a fresh set of clothes, Ryan sat in a lawn chair and from a safe distance watched the frenzied yellow jackets still swarming around the mower. He tapped the tank of gasoline by his side with a box of long-reach matches.

As the sun set, Ryan secured a headlamp above his brow and with the matches and gas in tow, crawled toward the hole. One by one, the yellow jackets glided into a nest that had been mulched to hell. Two remained, patrolling the Cub Cadet.

Ryan poured gasoline into the hole. He lit four matches and dropped them into the shallow depression and woooof! An orange ball of flame rose, illuminating the mower. The black and yellow-striped sentries descended into the blaze as if drawn by a beacon.

Ryan stretched out upon the terrace, smelled the mixture of fresh cut grass and gasoline and noticed how the dancing swirls of smoke blocked out some of the stars in the sky.

Make Me a Pallet (St. James Infirmary)

I slip on sunglasses to mask the black eye before hitting the lobby. Seven a.m., the security guard is gone and a new clerk is behind the front desk. "Hi," I say cheerfully, the early hours having left me no worse for wear. "Do you have a cell phone for me?"

"Room 223, yep, got it right here," he says.

"Thanks for the safekeeping."

"No problem. Have a good one."

I always hit the breakfast early, before the hordes descend, when the food is hot and the coffee fresh. A few retired, sightseeing couples, ready to hit the road and keep pace with the sun, are eating oatmeal and drinking tea.

Placing a day-old *USA Today* down, I stake claim to a two-top by the window. An attractive young woman is filling a bowl with hardboiled eggs. Her nametag says "Erica." There's a devious spark in her eye. Erica moves like an exotic dancer, her hips shoving air out of the way as she weaves in and out of tables, picking up a cup here, a plate there. A single wild streak of pink runs through her blond dye job and is strangled in a ponytail. Erica is a hellcat.

I drop off my coffee, two eggs, and a bagel, and fix a plate for Sophia: blueberry muffin, banana, and orange juice. The two businessmen I'd seen earlier this morning are dressed for golf. They take their coffee to the couch.

"Good morning," Sophia says, giving me a kiss before sitting down at our table. "Sunglasses are a nice touch. Blueberry, lovely. Thank you."

Her long, chestnut hair is down, which I love, and she wears a soft v-neck t-shirt which compliments her slender torso and tender breasts. Yoga pants hug her hips. I can't get into the yoga voodoo, but I love Sophia in the apparel.

Now it begins. They wander in, yawning and scratching their heads—teenagers—moppish hair and checked, cotton pajama bottoms; their mothers and fathers in identical pajama bottoms, wearing blue fluorescent Crocs.

Then the SCARE-A-CONS show up with the same gruesome wardrobe they were wearing when they returned this morning.

They are followed by gamblers who have doubled-down, taking advantage of La Quinta's complimentary breakfast before indulging in the casino's all-you-can-eat buffet. Worn-down types dragging oxygen tanks. Plastic debit cards, to be inserted into slot machines, are clipped to colorful telephone cords attached at their waists. After many years hunched over the one-armed bandits, necks have been absorbed by shoulders, now melded with skulls.

Between the gamblers, SCARE-A-CONS, and families, it's hard to distinguish the real zombies from the make believe.

I've forgotten Sophia's coffee. I'm able to slip in and pour a cup while the "slow-walkers" jockey for position around the waffle griddle, the rack of Fruit Loops and Frosted Flakes, and the microwave to nuke Jimmy Dean sausage biscuits.

"Thanks," Sophia says. She peels her banana very slowly, playfully. "So, what's her name?"

"Who?"

"The chick with the skunkish pink stripe in her hair," she says, her eyes darting to Erica, who is slinking her way to the waffle griddle.

The two businessmen are having trouble producing batter from what can only be described as an udder affixed to a metal vat. Erica smiles. With a firm grip, she fondles the udder. Batter slowly drips into a cup. "It's very thick today," Erica says. "It's usually not this thick."

I spread cream cheese on my bagel. "I haven't talked to her."

"Oh, come on," Sophia says. "When you see a party girl it

takes you five seconds to get her name. I know what you like."

"Erica."

"Thought you said you didn't talk to her?" Sophia says.

"I said I didn't talk to her. I never said that I didn't know her name; it's on her name tag."

"Erica," she says, drawing out the name in a husky voice as she bites into her banana. She skims the newspaper and says, "She looks like a good reason not to have a girlfriend—or a wife."

January

Faulkner knew about the past, something about the "past not being dead…not even past." But he must have known, no matter how close you get, you can never touch it.

Sam knew this. Nonetheless, on that cold afternoon, he rolled down Hollow Road, a narrow gravel lane no one had ever gotten around to paving. In his pricey Volvo sedan, he was many miles removed from the piece-of-shit robin-egg blue Ford Escort he used to drive up and down this road.

It had been eleven years since Sam had seen the little white cottage tucked in the woods of northern Baltimore that, in his college days, he shared with two women.

Sam was married, three years now, and he didn't know why he was driving down this road. Maybe he just didn't want to go Christmas shopping, which was what he was supposed to do while Debra, his wife, put in a few hours at the office.

•

Sam had lived in the house with his girlfriend, Lisa, an aspiring actress who had officially changed her last name at the age of eighteen from Crickenberger to Morgan, and her best friend, Celeste LaChance—also an aspiring actress with no need to change her name. The place came furnished with a sofa, coffee table, pinewood dining table, mountain bikes, and a canoe.

In addition to his two roommates, the two features that

attracted Sam most were a potbelly woodstove and the path through the woods that opened up to a reservoir. He'd heard that F. Scott Fitzgerald once owned a house nearby and that John Lennon had looked at property on the secluded body of water. He didn't know if any of that was true, but it sounded good.

It was an artistic abode that fueled the trio's interests in plays, poetry, painting, and photography. Since it was in the middle of nowhere it was also perfect for raucous parties.

One night, having consumed his quota of wine and whiskey, Sam stumbled into the darkness and sat on the hill next to the canoe. A woman was sitting there as well, a woman he thought was Celeste, a woman he'd always been attracted to. They crawled into the canoe.

By the time they put their clothes back on, Sam realized he did not know this woman. She was just as wasted. They went back into the house, where the party was still in full swing, acting as if nothing had happened.

That signaled the beginning of the end of Sam's idyllic cottage life.

•

The motor running, Sam sat there looking at the little cottage. No matter how badly it ended, he remembered being distinctly happy. Not that he was unhappy now; Sam was exceptionally happy. He was still young, had a beautiful wife, both had good jobs, a wonderful home, prospects of a child, perhaps, in the next year or two, and no chaos. Sam's life was very civilized.

His cell phone rang. It was Debra.

"Hi, what are you up to?" she said.

"Remember I told you I used to live around here, well, I'm sitting in front of the house."

"Okay." There was no tone of anger in her voice. "How'd the Christmas shopping go?"

"Listen, can we just do all our shopping online?"

"Sure, fine with me." There was no hint of annoyance in her voice. "You were the one who had the idea of shopping today."

"I know, I know," Sam said. "I'm going to park the car at your office and walk over to an Irish pub I used to go to and then I'll meet you at the party."

"Christmas spirit got you all nostalgic?" She said this in a frostier tone.

"Maybe, I guess."

"The party's at five. We don't have to stay long. It's supposed to snow tonight."

"Yeah, I heard on the radio. Love you."

"I love you, too," Debra said. "Still like being married?"

"Very much so. See you soon."

●

The Middle Eastern men huddled over laptops at the end of the bar suggested new ownership. Other than that, Sullivan's hadn't changed. Sam found a stool on the bend of the bar close to the door.

Not only was Sullivan's an Irish pub, it was a shrine to the late, great Johnny Unitas. Oil paintings and newspaper clippings depicting the legendary quarterback hung on the wall.

Inside the bathroom, urinals displayed the name "Bob Irsay" at the exact spot where one would aim to deposit the contents of their bladder. The reviled Colts owner had infamously moved the team in the middle of the night aboard Mayflower tractor-trailers to Indiana.

As Sam perused the top-shelf bourbons, the bartender, an older woman in her fifties, frosted hair, laid down a cocktail napkin.

"How are you?" she said.

"Just fine, you?" It felt good sitting alone in a pub on a

Friday afternoon with snow on the way.

"Never been better," she said. "What are you drinking?"

"Woodford Reserve, neat, please."

"You bet. Menu?"

"No thanks."

"Look at the size of that boar," a woman shouted.

A group in the middle of the bar was watching CNN. Breaking news: A wild boar was terrorizing a Southern California subdivision. Animal control and police officers with rifles had cornered the boar by a swimming pool. They moved in and literally hog tied the beast.

"They must've sedated that sonofabitch," said a man, sipping a pint of Guinness.

"Of course they sedated it," the bartender said over her shoulder as she delivered Sam's bourbon.

"Boar that size wouldn't put up with that," the man said.

"That's why they're called boars," the bartender said, laughing.

As the conversation moved from boars to the turf war in the swamps of Florida between alligators and invasive pythons, and whether or not animals were going crazy or just going animal, a group of young professionals with Christmas presents gathered at two round tables.

The women, three of them, were all put together but the four men were dressed down in khakis, button-down shirts with loosened ties and fleece zip-ups. They went to the bar and inundated the bartender with drink orders: beers, gin and tonics, tequila and fruity, exotic shots that required lots of vodka—drinks specifically designed for getting drunk.

Sam focused on one woman, a striking, tall blonde. She removed her red, velvet jacket to reveal a pleated, charcoal miniskirt and tight black, turtleneck sweater which amplified her breasts.

"January Jones."

Sam hadn't noticed the man sit down next to him. "Excuse me?"

"That woman you are staring at, she looks like January Jones," the man said, not looking up from his newspaper.

He was a large man; everything about him was large, his voice, his girth. Even his gray suit seemed large for such a large man.

With his palm, he pulled back his thinning gray hair exposing a deep widow's peak. He shook his *Baltimore Sun* and expanded it full length, high above his brows. His eyes scanned left to right, moving down vertically, giving each article a quick glance before advancing to the top of the next page.

He breathed heavy, sighed and snorted; sweat rose on his forehead and sometimes he panted. He readjusted his body upon the stool, trying to find the most comfortable position. Occasionally, he'd wiggle in his suit jacket and pull at his shirt collar. He'd cough, phlegm swimming in his throat for a moment until he could reach for a napkin, wipe his mouth, then manage to lean up and over to throw it in a trash can behind the bar.

The man had not ordered a drink, but a Miller Lite was delivered to him. He took a quick sip and said thanks, not looking up from the paper.

"Who is January Jones?" Sam said.

"Actress," the man said. "She's on that TV show, *Mad Men.*"

"Never seen it," Sam said. He finished his bourbon and continued to stare at the blonde, who politely smiled at a male co-worker who was attempting to engage her in a conversation.

"She's into sharks," the man said. "That's her cause, protecting sharks." He folded the paper and laid it down on the bar, giving his full attention to the sports section.

The bartender came by and asked Sam if he wanted another Woodford.

"Yes, please. Thank you."

The man looked up from the paper. "Derby bourbon."

"What's that?"

"Woodford—bourbon of the Kentucky Derby."

"Oh. Didn't know that," Sam said.

"My family used to be in the horse racing business. My daddy trained and bred thoroughbreds. Maple Run Farm, in the Worthington Valley—not far from here. Up the road from Sagamore where Native Dancer is buried."

"Native Dancer?"

"Magnificent horse. A lot of great thoroughbreds trace their bloodlines back to Native Dancer."

Sam offered the only thing he knew about horse racing: "I've been to the Preakness a few times."

A cheeseburger arrived in front of the man without him ordering. "Preakness," he said. "Circus. Half the people there don't even know a horse race is happening. Just drinking and dressing up for a show. Drunken idiots running across the tops of toilets in the infield."

The man lifted his bun and dumped a side of jalapeños on the burger; then he drenched it with ketchup. He cut the sandwich in half. "Limestone," he said, "good for making horse's bones strong and that bourbon you're drinking."

The man bit into half of the divided cheeseburger. He wiped away the ketchup dripping from the sides of his mouth.

Sam sipped his fresh bourbon.

"Limestone shelf runs through Worthington Valley," the man said. "My daddy told me if we couldn't breed horses, we could always make whiskey."

Sam pulled out his cell phone to check the time.

The man put his cheeseburger down. "Goddamn, I got to stop eating jalapeños—had a bellyache for a week."

He drank his beer and continued, "Anyway, the industry has gone down the drain: track owners, Jockey Club, and Annapolis—city of circles—have fucked it three ways to Sunday. That's why we got out."

The large man swallowed the remaining half of the half. Having wiped his hands, he reached into his jacket and held a card for Sam.

"We're in the beef business now. Local grass-fed Black Angus and bison wrapped and labeled. We'll see how long this whole 'buy-local' bubble lasts."

Sam put his phone down, knocked back a large swallow of Woodford, and took the card.

"Charlie Reynolds," the man said, extending a hand, ketchup wedged in two fingernails.

"Sam Butler," Sam said, shaking Charlie's hand. "Nice to meet you."

"Likewise," Charlie said. "Sam Butler. Now that's a hell of a name, just as Hollywood as January Jones."

Sam still had thirty minutes before he had to leave and was debating whether to have one more or just have a Coke and pay his bill. He compromised and ordered a Coke, a Woodford, and said, "I'll take my check, too."

Charlie wiped sweat from his cheek and put his head into his hands.

Sam's drinks arrived as he slid an empty glass toward the bartendar. He looked at Charlie. "Are you all right?"

"Yeah, fine."

"January Jones—she must have changed her real name," Sam said.

"Hey." Charlie called for the bartender.

"Yeah Charlie," she said.

"Can I please get a glass of water?"

"Sure thing," she said, grabbing a pint glass.

"Yes, that's her real name," Charlie said, coughing and clearing his throat. "Goddamn jalapeños. January Jones—her parents named her after a character in a novel."

"Well, she reminds me of a girl I dated in college. She wanted to be an actress—may be one now actually. She changed her last name from Crickenberger to Morgan."

Charlie took a gulp of water and sighed. "What's her first name?"

"Lisa," Sam said.

"Lisa Crickenberger to Lisa Morgan—smart move," Charlie said.

Charlie tipped his glass to Sam's wedding finger. "Guess you're not with Cricken-hopper or whatever her name is. How long you been married?"

"Three years," Sam said.

"Good for you." Charlie took another gulp of water and then asked for another. He bit down into the second half of his cheeseburger, swallowed, and grabbed some fries. "Sam, what do you do?

"I'm a photographer. If you ever go into those visitor centers on the highway, I take photographs for the magazines and brochures."

"Interesting," Charlie said. He drank his beer and another gulp of water and chomped into another portion of his cheeseburger. "Sam, take a look at January Jones and her friends."

Sam looked. The blonde and three of her male co-workers were throwing back shots of some green liquid. After they swallowed, all three giggled.

"All of these young people are looking for something," Charlie said.

"Love?" Sam said, putting back a large sip of Woodford, chased with Coke.

"Who knows," Charlie said. He finished the burger and drank his beer. He pulled at his collar and ate a few more fries and cleared his throat. "Those guys ordered girly drinks to display their sensitivity to January Jones—shooting back one of those dumbass fruity shooters is somehow endearing them to January Jones."

Charlie coughed and went red in the face.

"Are you all right?" Sam asked again.

"Yes, goddamnit."

Then Charlie grabbed Sam's Coke and took a drink.

Sam looked at Charlie and didn't know what to say. "Uh, I also knew a woman named Celeste LaChance. She wanted to be an actress too."

Charlie continued: "Men are supposed to drink drinks made for men. There's supposed to be a distance between men and women. The distance is there for a reason, therein lies the attraction—we're not supposed to understand it. How do we even begin to understand when the first clue we are given is the name January Jones—or Celeste LaChance?"

Charlie's body seized. He was in a great deal of pain. His eyes opened wide. He gritted his teeth and spit: "Goddamn jalapeños."

He slumped down on the bar knocking over the beer, his face falling into the ketchup and fries on his plate.

"Jesus Christ," the bartender said, coming from around the bar. "Is he choking?" she said to Sam, who stood and took a step back.

"I don't think so," he said.

"Well just don't stand there—help me get him on the floor. Call 911," the bartender shouted to the Middle Eastern men.

January Jones peered around the bend of the bar to see what was happening. One of her male co-workers rushed over and got on his knees. He opened Charlie's shirt and pressed into Charlie's chest with folded hands.

Sam didn't wait for the ambulance. He gave his money to one of the Middle Eastern men and left.

•

Sam met Debra at her party. He did not tell her about Lisa Crickenberger, Celeste LaChance, January Jones, Charlie Reynolds, or the incident at Sullivan's.

"Hi," Debra said, handing Sam a scallop wrapped in bacon.

"Hi."

"Angel on horseback," she said.

"What?"

"That's what these are called, angels on horseback."

"Oh," Sam said, giving a weak smile.

"How was your sojourn down memory lane?" Debra asked.

"Just fine," Sam said.

Make Me a Pallet
(Shave 'em Dry)

Inside the room, Sophia slams me against the door and rips open my shirt. Western snaps are convenient for such an aggressive advance. The belt is unbuckled and every piece of lower garment is stripped down to the ankles. Tongue glides over my chest, lips press against my ribs. She whispers, *Quiero tu leche.*

I don't know Spanish but believe she is saying something about needing my milk. Her cheek presses against my hip-bone and her compass is pointed south.

I raise her to my face. Her t-shirt is gone, Pumas kicked off, her yoga pants slipping away from her thighs, greased with lavender body oil, as I hop on one foot and then the other struggling with these cowboy boots, finally breaking free and tossing my denim across the room not giving a damn what might break.

She stands there. Her dimples deepen.

You can't get my honey without getting stung.

I fall to my knees, drowning where the Mississippi meets the Gulf. Sway to the desk, to the chair, holding onto her like timber cast off and floating down from Minnesota.

Upon the shore we're setting the woods on fire. I'm skipping, nose leading the way, turning curves, hopping through blazing thickets like Brer Rabbit, born from a briar patch.

I'll bring the coffee if you bring your cup.

I've got the biscuits let me sweeten your tea.

Sitting on top of the world, wailing hymns, kicking the sheets from the bed, flesh on the grill, give the dog a bone, tongues tangled like telephone wires in a hurricane, straddling the lightning, moving with no definition of geography, pumping the brakes, looking both ways at the crossroads, roses and thorns, spines like copperheads crawling from their nest, heads almost severed by sabers, begging mercy from ghosts at the banks of Devil's Backbone Creek.

Not an inch of this room is untouched.

Pressed Luck

"Pilgrims," she whispered. Helen watched from the hotel room as her husband packed their blue Chevy Tahoe. Oxford, Mississippi, was the last stop on a road trip to celebrate their tenth wedding anniversary. Helen and her husband, Jack, had joined thousands of motorists embarking on the autumn Natchez Trace Pilgrimage, a lazy Southern sojourn along a four-hundred-and-forty mile scenic parkway that stretched from Nashville to the Mississippi river town named for an Indian tribe that settled upon the banks of the "big muddy" in the 1500s.

Over the past week they had taken in the fiery foliage, toured antebellum mansions, consumed copious amounts of catfish, and sipped Mississippi Punch. Oxford was not along the Trace, but Helen wanted to see Rowan Oak.

When they arrived yesterday afternoon, Helen and Jack went straight to Old Taylor Road and pulled off at a hard curve and walked down the gravel lane to the residence William Faulkner called home for more than thirty years. They strolled through the mid-nineteenth century Greek Revival house, stopping to stare at Faulkner's pipe, his typewriter, his bedroom; but it was the author's outline for the novel, *A Fable*—handwritten on the walls of his office—that captured Helen's attention.

Roaming the grounds, Helen took pictures of the wisteria rising from the center of a circular wrought iron bench in the rose garden as Jack stood by the old kitchen trying to get a cell phone signal. Helen lingered in the soft southerly breeze, gazing at the magnolias and dogwoods, the Osage orange trees.

A burly biker parked his Harley and met Helen and Jack as they were returning to their Tahoe. He, too, had diverted from the Trace to visit Rowan Oak. Intimidating in size, frightening tattoos sleeving his arm, he spoke with the softest voice when he offered to take a picture of them in front of the house.

Smiling beneath the double row of red cedars leading to the front porch, Jack's arm casually draped over Helen's shoulder. Helen then asked the man if he would take a picture of just her; a photo that completed Helen's desire to detour.

•

Later that evening, they toasted ten years and dined on shrimp and grits at City Grocery. At the table next to theirs sat Morgan Freeman. At one point, the actor leaned over and whispered, "Congratulations." They thanked him but did not ask for an autograph.

When Helen and Jack left the restaurant they marveled at the sight of this tall, regal black man standing on the square, the elegant elder statesman of stage and screen—the voice of God—flanked by swooning petite blond debutants deep in the heart of the former Confederacy.

They walked back to the hotel. Once in their room, Jack poured Helen a glass of red wine. He had a glass of bourbon. They kissed. They got into bed. Arms moved around bodies, kisses were placed on shoulders and nipples and lips, every advance suggested lovemaking but eventually they fell asleep with the television on.

The next day Helen was thinking about Morgan Freeman when her husband walked into the room, having packed the Tahoe, dabbing sweat on his forehead with a handkerchief. It was mid-October but still very warm in Oxford. Jack looked at his new Timex watch, an anniversary gift from his wife (he gave her earrings). "All set?"

She walked up to her husband and brushed lint off his black polo shirt and smiled. "All set."

Eight hundred and sixty-three miles back home to Maryland.

●

They rejoined the Natchez Trace in Tupelo, birthplace of the "King of Rock 'n Roll." Not a single word had passed between them since they left Oxford. The music was turned down low, tuned to a blues station on their satellite radio. Helen was engrossed in a road map with decorated veins of pink and yellow and orange highlights, plotting a course upon the eight-thousand-year-old trail, the "Devil's Backbone"—carved and trampled upon by the bearded buffalo; the Choctaw and Chickasaw; Spanish Conquistadors, De Soto's futile search for gold; hearty pioneers propelled by an unwavering belief in Manifest Destiny, Davy Crocket-type-frontiersmen and thieving highwaymen.

"You know there's a whole country passing you by while you're looking down at that map," Jack said.

Helen took a deep breath. "There was a time when I didn't believe in you."

"What?"

She shook her head gently. "I wasn't sure about you. Had my doubts."

Helen looked down at the map and circled something with the pink highlighter. "When we get into Tennessee, I'd like to stop at the Meriwether Lewis Site. That's where he killed himself—or was murdered. His grave is marked with a broken stone. Symbolizes a life cut short."

She turned the air-conditioning off and rolled down the window and let her hand sail as the red-clay hills, devoured by kudzu, passed in the rearview mirror.

"What's this not-believing thing about?" Jack said.

"Yes," Helen said, neatly folding the map. "There was a

time when I had my doubts."

"Before or after we were married?"

She opened a bottle of water and took a sip. "Well, of course I had doubts before we were married. Why wouldn't I have doubts before we were married?"

Jack focused on the road.

"Even when we committed or you committed," she said.

"What the hell does that mean?" Jack shifted lanes, moving past a group of cyclists.

"All right, we. Relax."

"You make it sound as if you were the only one invested in a commitment, in a relationship," he said.

"Relax. Watch your speed. This road is notorious for speed traps," Helen said. "As I was saying, after we resolved that we were going to be together—marriage or no marriage—I wasn't sure I believed in you."

"Believe?" Jack said. "What, like Santa Claus?"

"I wasn't sure you were going to see this thing through."

Jack rolled up Helen's window and turned the air-conditioning back on.

"Before, you were so wild," she said. "Remember?"

"No."

"You don't remember being wild? I was so in love with you, and I knew you were in love with me but you were so crazy. You had a life I wasn't part of—the music, the late nights." She looked at him. "You don't remember that?"

"No."

"We were living together, sometimes dating, sometimes not dating. And let's be honest, all those other women. Good Lord."

"As I recall you had plenty of company," Jack snapped, turning the radio up.

"Thought you didn't remember—speed!" Helen said, pointing at the dashboard. She settled back in her seat. "I know I had plenty of company. I hate thinking about that period in our lives."

"You brought it up," he said.

"But yes, after we made the commitment I had my doubts, even after we got married."

"Why is that?"

"You had this terrible habit of pressing your luck." Helen took another sip of water.

"I have no clue what you are talking about."

"Blocked those days out, huh? Banished them to some dark closet?" Helen asked.

"I don't think about any of that, not any more."

"You believe in erasing the past? Like the day before never existed? Are you saying we woke up this morning as strangers? I mean, I understand that. I wake up sometimes and feel like a completely different person than the person I was the day before. Sometimes I look at you and for a split second I don't recognize you."

Jack readjusted the rearview mirror and turned the radio off and looked at Helen. "Were you drinking this morning?"

"Answer the question," she said. "Do you believe that you can erase the past?"

"Of course not."

"But you don't remember the past?" she said.

"Goddamnit, I don't know anything about the past. Why are you bringing this up?"

"I don't know," Helen said, turning the radio back on, the air-conditioning off, and rolling down her window. "You say we never talk when we take these road trips. So, now I'm talking."

Make Me a Pallet
(Fastest of Ponies)

I need cigarettes, and I need to get out of the La Quinta.

I break a sweat just walking to the Jeep. It's brutally hot and humid. It feels like there's a damp towel around my neck.

Up the road from the casino, I walk into a SavOn, a franchise also owned by the Oneida Nation. With no federal taxes levied, the cigarettes are cheap.

"Do you have American Spirits?" I ask a petite dark haired woman behind the counter. I have no idea if she is Native American or not.

"What are those?" she says refilling a rack of dream catchers and setting out a new sleeve of energy drink shots.

"They're cigarettes, no chemicals, natural."

"Nope, don't have them."

It strikes me odd as I picture the label with the silhouette of, well, an Indian smoking a peace pipe, thunderbird symbol above his headdress.

"Okay," I say. "Is there a place around here that might have them?"

"Try Nice n' Easy."

"What's that?"

"Gas station down the road, about seven miles, in Sherrill."

I don't mind a seven mile drive. Sometimes I purposely get turned around just for the sake of driving: Hancock, a hell of a long curve into Chattanooga, then a deep cut into the Cotton Belt, jackrabbit quick from Shamrock, Texas—home of Bill Mack, "the satellite cowboy," late night DJ keeping truckers awake while he's penning tunes recorded by Jerry Lee Lewis,

Ray Price, and the big hit, "Blue," warbled by that ole' pussy cat, LeAnn Rimes; pausing at rest stops outfitted with tornado shelters and before I know it—Tucumcari, and ghost motels along mythologized, weed sprouting Route 66; Las Vegas to L.A., no air conditioning, sweating out the dry heat of the Mojave, through Baker where the tallest thermometer in the lower forty-eight confirms one-hundred-and-eleven degrees, and up the Pacific Coast dining on fish tacos and breathing in the garlic fields.

I know every Wawa in the Mid-Atlantic; Cracker Barrels from Altoona to Terra Haute; TAs (Travel Americas) from Las Cruces to Coachella; Waffle Houses from Cornith to Ocala. Give me twenty-four hours anywhere and I can give you directions.

I'm about to walk into the Nice n' Easy and a man pumping gas asks if I know how to get to Turning Stone. I say, "Just up the road, seven miles on the right, you can't miss it."

I purchase American Spirits and a pack of gum.

The round Latino woman at the register is having trouble ringing up my items. "My fingers are not working today," she says.

I pick up a Bic lighter with a picture of a goat and the word "Capricorn," my astrological sign. "Throw this in, too, please."

"Goat," she says, chuckling.

"Yes," I say, removing my sunglasses to reveal my black eye. "It's my sign."

She stops laughing and scans the lighter and gives me my total.

"Jesus was a Capricorn," I say, as she hands me my change.

"Jesus Christo," she says.

"Sí, Jesus Christo."

Before I drank the Woody Guthrie/Jack Kerouac Kool-Aid, I'd studied Lewis and Clark's expedition and the opening of the West; John Smith's boat ride up the Chesapeake in search of the Pacific Ocean; I knew of Alvar Núñez Cabeza de Vaca's eight-year ramble from Florida to the Southwest.

In 1528, shipwrecked and abandoned, the Spanish Conquistador "wandered lost and naked through many and very strange lands" absorbing the new world and its inhabitants. A slave to natives, a refugee turned trader turned faith healer, subsisting, at times, only on the juice of the "prickly pear" as he roamed.

Cabeza de Vaca sailed home to Spain with La Relación, an account of his journey, "…the only thing that a man who returned naked could bring back."

I'm thinking about a line from La Relación when I stop at a liquor store on the way back to the La Quinta. "Freedom to go wherever I wanted…obligated to nothing and was not a slave."

Placing a fifth of Wild Turkey on the counter, I reach into my pocket and hand the pale-faced, wiry man a fifty-dollar bill. He is missing his two top-left incisors and the small tuft of red hair gives him the look of a sickly rooster.

"Yes sir, yes sir—Wild Turkey. What are you up to today?" he says, as if I'm his neighbor, which I guess is true, at least for the weekend.

"Just taking it easy."

"Just taking it easy, yes sir. Ah, Moses, gonna be another hot one," he says, looking over my head. He's watching the Weather Channel as he hands me my change.

"I gave you a fifty."

"Ah, Moses, you're right." He corrects his mistake. "What are you up to today?" he says again.

"Just taking it easy."

"Yes sir, heard that. Wild Turkey, that's a man who knows what he's doing. Taking it easy."

Awash

After more than forty years of marriage, Danny and Ellen were still talking.

They dug their flip-flops into the sand, following two redheads in their late teens. Danny recognized the identical twins. They were their neighbor's granddaughters visiting from Minnesota.

The boys on the beach stopped kicking a soccer ball around and gazed, glassy-eyed, mouths hung open, at the young ladies in bikinis, their healthy skin and hair the color of cherry soda pop.

Danny appreciated beauty but stopped looking at other women that way when he first met his wife at the Classic Cruiser's Tavern in the Hamptons.

All these many moons gone by, Danny and the boys would go for cocktails at the clubhouse after nine-holes and he'd listen to the men talk in lurid ways about young women they'd seen shopping at the Publix. All Danny could say: "I don't go out for hamburgers when I have steak at home."

•

They were in a good mood when they put their feet in the Gulf of Mexico. Since retiring to Bradenton seven years ago, there was rarely a day of unhappiness. Their children, a daughter in Baltimore and a son in Buffalo, were married with kids of their own. Leaving their home on Long Island, Danny and Ellen were now content to reinvent themselves as Floridians.

This day, however, was filled with added excitement. Tonight the clubhouse was holding their annual talent show and Danny had entered. He'd be singing the 1940s hit ballad, "You Belong to Me." His blue, pinstriped suit was dry cleaned; he was well rehearsed having performed the song on many occasions at a nearby tiki bar's karaoke night, the phrasing perfected as he showered in the morning.

Neither of them were good swimmers so they'd wade in to where the water reached their waists. Danny took hold of Ellen and danced with her through the gentle waves, crooning: "See the pyramids along the Nile, watch the sunrise from a tropic isle, just remember, darling all the while, you belong to me," closing with, "bub-bub-ba-do."

Ellen interrupted Danny's goofing and asked him a serious question: "Danny, I don't feel the bottom any more, do you?"

He assessed his position. "Uh—no."

Danny and Ellen had been caught in a riptide. They looked at the beach, now at least a quarter-mile away. Since it was a private beach there were no lifeguards and signs read, "Enter the water at your own risk."

They tried to swim, but couldn't. They flailed their arms; their heads dipping below, swallowing salt water. They screamed and the more they screamed the salt ripped their throats causing blood to come out of their mouths.

After several minutes of pleading to a distant shore, Ellen told Danny, "We have to float on our backs and get our heads together."

After she said this, she began preparations, resolving that this may be it; that having beaten breast cancer, Danny surviving a heart attack, this is how it was going to end, washed away in the Gulf of Mexico. What a way to go, a fate she never saw coming, but then again, you never do see it coming no matter how much you prepare.

Ellen began to cry. She couldn't compose herself but tried to make a joke. "Guess we're not going to the talent show tonight?"

Danny's belly, in full blossom after many years of good eating, buoyed up and down. His arms made soft, tranquil strokes, as if he were floating in a swimming pool. He reached out and took Ellen's hand. "Did I ever tell you about Johnny Gentry," Danny said casually, the way he would start a conversation when they lounged on their lanai.

"What? Who? Johnny Gentry—no."

"When I was working at Western Electric in Queens, before I met you, I knew this guy, Johnny Gentry. Now, this was Halloween, had to be 1961. They were having a costume contest at the Knights of Columbus—the prize was one-hundred dollars. My brother Don was going to go with his girlfriend, Patty. He cooked up these costumes—he was a plug and she was a socket and he had the whole thing wired so that when they danced and plugged into each other, light bulbs attached to their heads would light up. And Mark Wilder, who we called 'Nipper' because he was always taking nips of Scotch throughout the day, he worked at the funeral home and was going to borrow a coffin and have someone wheel him in to the party."

Ellen felt the sun move through her skin. She sank below the water's surface to escape the burning rays. She emerged and found herself standing again, but the shore seemed farther away. "Danny," she said.

"Ellen, just let me tell you this story."

"Danny, shut-up and stand up."

"I can't stand. I'm floating out into the middle of the Gulf of Mexico."

"Just stand. We must be on a sandbar or something."

Danny stood, water slapping at his chin. He looked around. "Well, I guess this is a bit of an improvement."

A thought entered her mind, a thought she had overlooked. "What about sharks?"

Picking up where he left off, Danny said: "So, anyway, Pete Taylor, Joey O'Brien, and I decide to go as the characters from *The Wizard of Oz*. Pete was big and had red hair so he was the

Lion, Joey was the Scarecrow, and I went as the Tin Man—"

"Danny."

"What?" he said, annoyed.

"Sharks."

"What about them?"

"There are sharks in the Gulf of Mexico."

"Why don't we pretend there aren't?"

"What?"

"Can I please finish my goddamn story?"

Danny rarely raised his voice. Granted, this was a unique predicament. Ellen stared at him, dumbfounded.

"Johnny Gentry," Danny continued, "rented a basement apartment from Joey's mother. He was into theatre, so he helped us pull together some costumes and did all our make-up. We were pretty sure we were going to win. Don and Patty's costumes—half the people going to the party were electricians and any one of them could have wired a get-up. All Nipper did was get inside a coffin and have someone roll him in. But we looked like the characters from *The Wizard of Oz*. So, we get there and Johnny shows up dressed as a woman and he looks really, really good. He looks like a woman. He could have used the ladies room and no one would have said anything. Johnny was always a little effeminate, but back then the word 'gay,' you know, meant you were happy. Johnny was six-foot-one and no one was going to say anything to him. He'd been in the Marines and he'd just crush you. Anyway, he won the contest."

"Why the hell did you just tell me that story?"

"I don't know." Danny laid back and floated again. "I just remembered I'd never told you that story."

"Take hold of this," a woman's voice said.

Danny opened his eyes. One of the twins had swum out with a boogie board. "Grab hold of this so you can float," she said, her voice bright with no sense of alarm.

Ellen started to cry again. "Bless your heart, oh God, thank you, thank you. You have such beautiful, long red hair. And what's your name?"

"Trish," she said smiling.

"Where did you learn to swim?"

"Minnesota," Trish said. "We do have water up north. My sister went for help."

•

A paramedic from the water rescue patrol brought all three to shore aboard a jet ski. After a short visit to the ER, Ellen and Danny returned home. They did not go to the talent show.

Instead, Danny made two drinks: vodka—hers with a slice of lemon, his with olives. Still in their bathing suits, they went back to the beach. The sun was setting and they didn't say a word.

Make Me a Pallet
(Tender Maidens)

I'm in the elevator, heading down to meet the van for tonight's show, accompanied by six blond beauties in black miniskirts. Each giggling one of them is holding a bottle of Corona. Brides-maids, I'm guessing. I stand in the back with the tackle box and amp and can't help but stare at their exposed spines.

On the sidewalk, like me, they wait for their ride. Smart phones are passed around for photos.

"Would you like me to take a picture of all of you together?" I ask.

This makes them very happy and they clap their hands and jump up and down in their miniskirts and high heels. One at a time, they hand me their phones.

A red Chevy Suburban pulls up behind me. Two old, weathered fly fishermen step out and unload their equipment, occasionally giving the women a glance.

After I've snapped a shot, I say, "Let's do one more."

One of the fly fishermen goes into the hotel, while the other lights a cigar. Photos taken, phones returned—each lady gives me a kiss on the cheek. The last one plants her moist mouth to my lips. Their limo arrives and they wave as they pile in, still holding their beers.

"Nice work," the fisherman says. "Lucky man. They all yours?"

Ripple Meets the Deep

No hug. No handshake. Not even a simple hello.

"Thought you were arriving yesterday and staying the night," Randall said.

The scrawny yellow dog barked at Wayne, as he stood in his father's driveway.

"Shut-up Jubal," Randall said. The dog sat and looked up at his owner and then at Wayne and then into the yard at nothing in particular.

"Still naming your dogs after Civil War generals?" Wayne said.

"Yep. So? What's the story?"

"I lost steam on the way up here and stayed at a Best Western in LaVale."

"You should have called," Randall said.

"I did call. I left a message."

"I didn't get a message."

Wayne had been through this before with his father. He didn't press the issue. It was futile. "Sorry for the miscommunication."

"Well, I'm glad you picked up the phone this morning," Randall said.

"I knew what time we were leaving." Then Wayne decided to press the issue: "I said I would be here."

"All right, fine. It doesn't matter. You got your fishing license, right?" Randall said.

"Yes."

"I see you're wearing Pac Boots like I told you. Main thing out there is not to get wet."

•

Wayne hadn't seen his father in over a year. In the last twelve
months, Randall's chocolate lab, Buford, had died and his
second wife, a Filipino woman named Lydia—twenty years
younger than Randall—had left him. Wayne was in no
position to decline the invitation to go ice fishing on Deep
Creek Lake. He'd never been ice fishing before, but the
prospect of sitting all day on a frozen body of water did not
entirely swell enthusiasm.

It was the weekend before Valentine's Day and, as was
typical of Maryland's bi-polar winter weather patterns, the
state was experiencing a warm spell. When Wayne left his
Chestertown home on the Eastern Shore, where he taught
history at Washington College, temperatures were in the mid-
sixties and had only dropped a few degrees when he reached
Cumberland.

By the time he got to his father's home in McHenry,
the thermometer hovered around forty degrees. Snow still
covered the ground.

Garrett County, west of the Eastern Continental Divide and
part of the Mississippi Watershed—not the Chesapeake—was
as far south and east as one could go to do serious ice fishing,
but some winters could bring only slush to the four-thousand
acre, man-made lake. Other seasons, however, had produced
twenty inches of solid ice giving an angler the feeling that he
was fishing atop a glass table.

Fishing at St. Patrick's Day, Wayne's father had told him,
that's when you had it really good.

•

Just after six in the morning, the moon still hanging in the sky
with the sun rising in the East, the three of them, father and
son, Jubal in the middle, took off in Randall's pickup truck
headed for the "super secret fishing spot," as Randall called it.

They looked like an advertisement for Bass Pro Shop.

Randall was not a talker. He was prickly, easily agitated and had not mellowed in his 60s. Wayne made the decision before he arrived that he would not initiate a conversation unless the moment absolutely presented itself. In the past, idle chatter when they were together only resulted in more prolonged periods of silence. It was better to speak only when spoken to.

However, after a few miles of driving, Wayne seized on a topic he felt might have traction. "Where'd you get Jubal?" he said.

The dog pricked his ears and looked at Wayne, his tongue hanging out.

"I found him online. He's a rescue. Went down to South Carolina to get him."

"That's a long haul for a dog," Wayne said.

"Not that bad. Worth it." Randall scratched the back of Jubal's neck, his eyes still on the road. "Spent ten minutes with him and I was convinced. They found him wandering around some railroad tracks scavenging for food. When I got him home he ate so damn fast I had to put a metal ball in the bowl to slow him down. Probably thought it might be his last meal."

Wayne stared out the window. Log homes sat off the road, hemmed in by thick woods suggesting a rugged, frontier lifestyle, but these houses started at $400,000 and were designed with every amenity found in civilization. "What's the mix?" Wayne said.

"Mix?" Randall gave Wayne a look as if he'd just been insulted. "Jubal's a Carolina Dog."

"A what?"

"A Carolina Dog."

"He looks like a dingo," Wayne said.

"He is. This particular breed is also known as the American Dingo. They live out in the wild."

"Well, if he's wild, he's got to be some kind of mix," Wayne said.

"Well, uh, Carolina Dogs can have all kinds of bloodlines."

"So, essentially he's a particular breed of mutt."

Randall bristled: "If you want to be crass about it."

•

Randall and Wayne turned down a dirt road and arrived at a spot that opened to a wide swath of Deep Creek Lake, the shoreline bordered by hemlocks, spruces, red and white pines. Tucked in the cradle of Savage to the north, Backbone to the south, the clouds left shadowed bruises upon the mountains, three-thousand feet above sea level.

A pair of polarized, mirrored sunglasses hung around Randall's neck and he placed a deer-skin, leather bomber hat, trimmed with red fox fur on his head.

"That your lucky fishing hat?" Wayne asked.

Randall sniffed and handed Wayne a pair of waterproof, insulated bib-overalls. "Here, put these on. And here." He handed Wayne a pair of gloves.

"I have gloves."

Randall placed a camouflage, Thinsulate lined life jacket on Jubal.

"You can't have equipment malfunctions out here," Randall said. "A simple thing like a knee cramp and you're done. You've got to have a pair of backup gloves, then you've got to have the ultimate pair of gloves when you're hands are about ready to die."

Wayne surveyed the gear in two sleds. "Don't you have one of those pup-tent type things—some kind of hut? Little gas stove to cook up chili and that kind of shit?"

"Shanty?" Randall said.

"Whatever it's called."

"I have one, but I don't use it when I'm fishing with other people. It's unsociable."

"Sociable" was not a word Wayne had ever associated with

his father.

Randall gave Wayne three heat packs. "I've got two thermoses of coffee. Also brought some 'anti-freeze' so we've got that covered."

"Anti-freeze?"

Randall reached into a backpack and produced two green, Stanley flasks. He shook them, smiled and winked. "Irish whiskey. Warm you right up."

•

Randall pulled the cord on the gas powered auger and cut ten holes, ten-feet apart, drilling through nineteen inches of ice, slushy water bubbling onto the lake's surface.

Trying not to slip, Wayne followed with the tip-ups, round discs that resembled landmines. A baited line was dropped from the tip-up. When a fish hit, an orange flag sprung up.

Placing the tip-ups over the holes, Randall said, "A lot of people think this is a blue collar kind of slumming because the fish are catching themselves."

Wayne watched Jubal gingerly circle the two of them in an agile trot. "Did you ever take Buford out here?"

"Goddamn disaster," Randall said. "Took him once. Silliest thing I've ever seen, that big, brown dog sliding all over the ice."

"I was sorry to hear about his passing."

Randall walked past Wayne. Jubal followed. "Old Buford was eighteen; that's something like one hundred in human years. Blind in one eye, old dog lungs. He knew it was coming, just kept looking out the window, like he wanted to disappear into the woods."

Randall handed Wayne a wooden box. "That's what they do when they're about die, just walk away. Cooked him a steak and he hung on for another week. Anyway, let's get you set up."

Jubal laid down on a pillow in one of the sleds. Randall

emptied the contents of a plastic bucket and turned it upside down in front of Wayne's hole. Randall had a black box with dials and a radar screen. A long wire, attached to the box, had a hockey puck-looking disc at the end. Scooping slush from the hole with a plastic spoon, Randall dropped the wire into the abyss and turned the box on. Adjusting dials, myriad colors appeared.

A crunching noise came from within the ice.

"What was that?" Wayne said. "It sounded like cracking."

"Just fracturing," Randall said.

"Aren't they the same thing?"

"Yes."

Randall continued, ignoring his son's concern. "This is your flasher."

Wayne peered down around his feet looking for splintering ice. "What's a flasher?"

"It's a fish finder." Randall's voice grew giddy. "I tell you, there's so much cool shit out there. Ice fishermen are real gear junkies. We use the word 'covet' quite frequently. 'I covet your fish finder; I covet your Pac Boots.' Hand me that box."

Inside were two lightweight fishing rods, only about two-feet long. Randall took a rod and dug into a container of mealworms. "These are St. Croix jigging poles," he said, baiting the hook and then dropping the line into the hole. "Best in the world. Come from Wisconsin."

Randall delicately bobbed the pole and said, "We'll try mealworms for a while and then move on to minnows if we're not getting any bites."

Staring into the flasher's screen, Randall signaled Wayne to come closer. "All right, we're hunting the big four: Northern Pike, Walleye, Yellow Perch, and Blue Gill. This section of the lake is a channel, between ten and twenty-two feet deep. You always want to fish on the transitions, where the ripple meets the deep.

Wayne smiled. His father was playing the role of "The Father," a role he never thought his father was altogether comfortable with. "Okay, transitions, got it."

"Yeah," Randall said. "We want to be where the shallow hits a big drop off. Fish like to hang out around that transition."

Randall got up and gave the pole to Wayne as he took a seat on the bucket.

"You're going to flutter this jig up and down to entice one of them big sonofabitch Northern Pike when they come through here," Randall said. He pointed to the screen. "The green thing, that's your lure and the red is the bottom. All of a sudden, a big red blob is going to come out from the bottom and nail it. That will be the fish."

Wayne fluttered the rod as instructed and saw something on the screen. "What's that yellow thing coming up from the bottom?"

Jubal scampered over from his pillow and stuck his snout into the hole.

"See how sensitive this thing is? That's a little fish looking at the bait. He's sniffing but he ain't ready to show up yet."

Picking up another bucket, Randall said, "Think you can handle it from here? I got to get jiggy with it."

"Jiggy with it?"

"You just watch that flasher."

"Shouldn't we be quiet?

"Why, they can't hear us. We're sitting on nineteen inches of ice," Randall said, pulling a sled toward his hole. Jubal followed.

•

Randall had been chatty while setting Wayne up; now that he was staring down into his own hole, Jubal asleep, he'd fallen into silence. Occasionally, he'd call in a robotic voice.

"You marking any fish?"

Each time, Wayne answered, "No."

An hour had gone by and except for Wayne's little yellow

blob, there'd been nothing lurking below, in the deep or the ripple.

Wayne took off his gloves and opened a thermos, allowing the steam to travel through his fingers and up into his face. He poured coffee, which gave him a lift.

He fluttered the rod and attempted to make the pole an extension of his arm. He let his mind go so that there was no thought, only instinct. When he found that existential place he was no longer self-conscious about idle chatter.

"How did you learn all this ice fishing stuff?" he said.

"Huh." Randall was startled, as if woken from a nap, which would not be unusual.

After Randall divorced Wayne's mother, he and his sister would visit their father every other weekend at his new home in Shepherdstown, across the Potomac in West Virginia. Often Randall would doze off at the wheel crossing back over South Mountain to take the kids home to Frederick. He'd drive sometimes a half-mile in what seemed a deep sleep. Wayne and his sister stopped waking him, unless they were drifting into another lane, because their father would get angry when they did. Wayne, as a boy, always said a prayer: "Please car, know how to drive yourself back home."

"What did you say?" Randall said. Jubal lifted his head momentarily, and then tucked his nose beneath his paws.

"How'd you get into ice fishing?"

"Five years ago when I moved here, I met some folks who ice fish. Guess it was my second winter, they invited me out. Fell in love with it. Not sure why."

Scooping slush from the hole, Randall said, "I'm switching to minnows."

Wayne reeled in his line and did the same.

"You know, during bass season, everyone gets tightlipped. It's very competitive," Randall said, "But ice fishing, it's very jovial, a lot of backslapping out here, a lot of conversation, sharing ideas."

Randall baited his line and said, "I don't hang out much,

but I had some guys who really took me under their wings. These fellas used to come out to this very spot—thirty or forty years ago—with ball peen hammers, screw drivers, and broom sticks and catch sixty perch in a morning. All their fishing gear came from hardware stores. That's old school."

"Well, I'll say this about ice fishing," Wayne said. "At least you don't need a boat. You can walk all over this lake."

Jubal stood, ears pricked, and barked. The sound of high-pitched engines bounced off the ice and echoed through the trees. Speeding down the channel were four snowmobiles.

"Oh hell," Randall said. "We have only one natural enemy out here and that's assholes on snowmobiles. They hate us because we drill these holes that freeze over and create speed bumps and we hate them because it feels like you're fishing on the Baltimore beltway."

The group circled Wayne and Randall and Jubal dug in, growling, defending their territory. Giving their machines gas, the riders sped off, skimming the ice around a bend in the lake.

The roar and smell of gasoline subsided and Randall said, "They're like coyotes and we're the sheep."

Randall checked his flasher as he lowered his line.

Wayne did nothing with his rod, just laid it down on the ice and rubbed his gloves together. "Dad, you want to talk about Lydia?"

"No, and don't bring it up again."

"Thought this was a conversational hobby," Wayne said.

"Well, why don't you bring up a topic that is worthy of conversation?"

"I swear to Christ, sometimes you come so close and then you just slip back into being an asshole. What the hell have we been talking about? Dead dogs, fish finders, fishing with screwdrivers from hardware stores—transitions?"

Jubal barked and made for Wayne. For a second, he thought the dog was going to attack him; then Randall pointed, "Wayne, to your right, flag."

The tip-up had been sprung. Jubal arrived to the orange flag before Randall or his son could get up off their buckets.

Wayne moved to the tip-up.

Randall, stepping delicately as not to slip in his excitement, said, "Just pull that line up slowly."

Wayne was holding a small Blue Gill, barely hooked, the minnow only half-bitten.

Randall got to the tip-up and grabbed the fish, removed the hook and hurled it across the ice.

Returning to his hole, Randall checked his watch.

Jubal sat next to Wayne. Randall didn't look over but called: "Jubal."

The dog reluctantly stood and trotted over to his master. "How close to what?" Randall said.

Wayne picked up his rod and punctured a mealworm with his hook and slipped the line into the water. "So close to being someone you'd actually like to talk to."

Reaching into a knapsack, Randall produced the flasks. He stuffed one into his jacket and slid the other in Wayne's direction. "Maybe I deserved that and maybe I didn't. I have absolutely no interest in psychoanalysis."

"I'm sorry Dad. That was out of line."

"Forget about it." Randall rubbed the back of Jubal's neck and said, "How is your mother?"

Wayne coughed out a laugh and shook his head. "Uh, she is fine."

"She still got the house?"

"Yes," Wayne said, tossing the flask into the sled. He resumed fluttering.

"Your sister? Hardly hear from her. Phone call here and there. I send her emails. She never responds."

Half-ignoring his father, "Yes," Wayne said. "She's still got the stable in Thurmont; boarding, lessons. Still doing the therapeutic riding."

"Well, that's good."

"Yep," Wayne said.

Randall adjusted his flasher. He bit a glove off and pulled the flask from his pocket, and unscrewing the cap with his thumb and index finger, Randall said: "You were always your mother's son. I always said the two of you would never get lost in a grocery store; same nose, same eyes, same blond hair. She used to cut your hair. Till you were five, you could have been the model for Dutch Boy paint. You were about to go into kindergarten or first grade. I told your mother, 'With that haircut he is going to get treated unmercifully, not only by boys, but girls too.' One Saturday, you and I went down to Gene's Barber Shop and I told Gene, 'Crop it tight around the sides, a little off the top, parted on the left.'"

"I remember that," Wayne said. He stared off to the edge of the bank where a six-point buck moved slowly. A gust of wind kicked up a layer of snow off the ice and the buck disappeared. "Yeah, I remember Gene's. Had a Coke machine that opened like a coffin. Had to put your money in and drag the glass bottle through slots and pull it out."

"Glass bottles," said Randall. "Didn't think they still had glass bottles when you were five, back when they made Coke out of sugar, none of that high fructose whatever. Anyway brought you home and your mother cried; you would have thought I had enlisted you in the army."

Randall took a sip from the flask. He reached into a zip-locked bag. He held out four dog treats. Jubal walked over and gobbled them in one swallow.

Giving the tip-ups a glance, Randall looked up at the sky. Clouds were clearing and the sun lit up the ice. "Do you remember the Pinewood Box Derby?" Randall said, taking another swig.

Wayne found his sunglasses and slipped them on. "Cub Scouts, fourth grade, yeah I remember."

"Your mother and I had just gotten the divorce and, well, that was a weird time for all of us."

"Weird? That's not the word I would use, but okay," Wayne said.

"I thought building that block of wood into a car would be a way we could reconnect. You won every race. You won the county title. We could have gone to the state meet. But you didn't want to go. Didn't even want to get pizza afterwards—just wanted to go home. I've still got your trophy if you want it. Got it back at the house."

"Nope, you keep it."

"I thought that was a starting point for trying to understand each other. You were pretty young when all that happened."

Wayne went for the flask but chose the thermos of coffee. "There were years before the divorce for us to get off on the wrong foot. Don't bring up Cub Scouts, and as for understanding, there was nothing to understand. Everyone went about their business. You and Mom got married, had two kids, got divorced and life went on. Why are you bringing this up? None of it matters now."

Wayne leaned into the sled and grabbed the flask and set it next to the flasher. "I'm wondering if this is what you meant by 'backslapping.'"

Gusts spun down the channel. Father, son, and dog—not even a yip from the American Dingo—looked up at a bald eagle flying low like an aircraft coming in for a landing, its six-foot wing span steady, rear feathers down as it glided in, its two talons grasping the littered Blue Gill. The bird ascended and veered left into a cluster of spruces, finally landing in its nest.

Randall opened his mouth but didn't say anything. He possessed the vocabulary, but the language was foreign to him when it came to discussing one's reaction to another human being, where all that was intangible, left without fingerprints, was beyond reason, unpredictable, when numbers were not available and mathematics were submerged in the slush, stifled below the surface, the science of emotional expression unexplained. He could not say: "Ah, Wayne, this is why I do it. Look at that bird. 'Thank you, God.' That's a moment many people don't get to see." He wasn't going to say to his son, that at this point, at his age, he felt compelled to sit on a frozen lake for penance, for mistakes and missed opportunities to make things right, redirect the course. Hell, it was not religion that he had found, but sitting by yourself, on a frozen lake, looking for a fish inside a dark ten-inch hole—yes, that gave a man time to think.

Wayne fluttered his rod as he watched the eagle. He couldn't remember if he blamed his father for anything and there was no forgiveness. Resolve and acceptance were more in line with Wayne's point of view. He would never be able to change what happened. His father had not abandoned him— "leaving" and "abandoning" were two different words.

He and his father were together today. What if one of them fell through the ice and the other had to save the other's life? Today would be today and a new chapter would begin. The past would be gone.

It was not lost on Wayne that, as a professor of history, he made a living off of the past. But it wasn't his. History, in part, was fiction.

•

Randall stood and stretched his arms, bent his back, moved his torso side to side. "Jubal my friend, I believe it is time to call it a day."

Jubal popped out of his pillow, knowing a fire was waiting at home and perhaps a biscuit.

"Let's wrap it up. If it was about catching fish, they'd call it catching," Randall said, lifting his flask. "Wayne, I'm proud of you."

Sometimes it's only five words. Wayne lifted his flask.

"People who don't like ice fishing are people who are always in search of something," Randall said. "They don't think sitting still is any fun. I ain't searching for anything."

They both drank.

Randall laughed, took another swig. The Western Maryland wind tickled the hairs of the red fox fur cap.

Wayne put the flask down and began to reel in his line, still scanning the flasher.

A big red blob came in not from the bottom but from the top. He pulled and the rod bent perpendicular to his wrist. He lowered the pole and reeled; fluttering became dunking.

He said nothing to his father, who was busy packing. But Jubal raced across the ice without a whisper and stood by the hole, alert, and trembling, not from cold but anticipation.

Wayne leaned back, sweat steaming from his forehead. A forty-inch Northern Pike surfaced, slapping violently. Wayne almost fell on his ass but spread his legs to balance himself.

Now Jubal started barking.

Randall turned. He ripped off his sunglasses. "Holy shit. Wayne, I'm coming."

Wayne had the slimy green monster by its gills with one hand and pulled off a glove with his teeth.

His father slipped and fell on his face but quickly crawled to his son.

Wayne reached into the fish's mouth to retrieve the hook. When he pulled his hand out it was dripping with blood, the flesh marked with slashes producing more blood that made the ice look like a bizarre candy cane.

"What the hell did you do that for? They have teeth!" Randall shouted.

His face turning white, Wayne said, "I didn't know that."

"You're a goddamn professor, don't you do research?"

Wayne dropped the pike, which flopped and rolled upon the ice like it had been set on fire.

Randall dove and grabbed the tail but the fish broke loose. He reached again, only far enough for his fingertips to scrape the bony midsection.

Jubal bit down on the pike's neck and it thrashed and whipped, its fine, razor teeth trying to rip into another wild animal. Jubal's four paws slipped and the pike broke free. It slithered its way back into the hole.

Randall heaved himself onto the hole, reaching down, searching through the dark, slushy water.

Make Me a Pallet
(Gone Fishin')

A family arrives at 1 a.m. The father wears khakis and a Hawaiian shirt, the vibrant Polynesian flowers replaced by 1950s red and blue Corvettes and Thunderbirds interspersed with Route 66 signs. The mother and daughter are dressed in identical black Under Armour warm-up suits.

The father is engaged in a serious dialogue with the desk clerk who taps away at his keyboard. Either there's a problem with their reservation or they haven't made one at all. Exhausted, the wife leans against the desk; her elbow rests on the counter, fist pressed into her cheek, cheap flip-flops revealing orange toenail polish.

While her parents sort out the situation, the daughter looks over the various snacks available for purchase, auburn ringlets bouncing as she bobs to some tune inside her head. She carries an old, brown leather briefcase.

She wanders into the lounge where I'm sitting.

"Hello," she says, not looking at me but at the plasma screen.

"Hi." I try not to be too engaging.

She turns and examines me as if I were an exhibit at a museum of natural history.

The credit card the father has given to the clerk is denied. He fumbles through his wallet for another piece of plastic.

The girl takes a seat next to me. "I've never been fishing. What kind is that?"

"Bass, large mouth," I say.

Mark Zona, host of *Zona's Awesome Fishing Show*, holds the fish by its gills. "Look at this beauty," he says, shoving its broken face toward the camera.

"You must fish a lot," the girl says.

"What makes you think that?"

"You have a tackle box."

My harmonica/tackle box is sitting next to her briefcase.

"Yeah, I fish a lot," I say, as Zona returns the bass to its home in a Louisiana lake.

"Why did you just lie to me?" she says.

I turn and stare directly into her freckled face and serious green eyes.

"Who are you?"

"Bridget," she says, extending her hand.

I give a gentle shake but offer no name.

"So, what's in the tackle box?"

"Why do you think I'm lying to you?" I slide over a bit to create distance.

"I saw the way you looked at the tackle box and then looked at me. Your eyes got shifty. Blue eyes are good for guilty-eye reading."

"Watch a lot of *Law and Order*?"

"*Mentalist*. What's your name, Mr. Secrets?"

"Travis."

"Travis? I wonder if that's like Travers, which means 'transverse, from the crossroads.' I know a lot about names and their meanings. Do you know what Bridget means?"

"Haven't a clue." I don't know what is happening here. I look over at the front desk and Bridget's parents have vanished.

"It's Irish," she says. "It means 'strength, strength to accept or strength to resist.' And there's Brigitte Bardot, the French actress, although our names are spelled differently."

"Bridget, how old are you?"

"Thirteen."

"And where are your parents?"

"Probably doing something in the room—usually doesn't take long. One of them will come down and get me."

"They don't mind that you are down here talking to a complete stranger at one o'clock in the morning?"

"No. I'm sure they told the desk clerk and that greasy looking security guard to keep an eye on us."

I crane my neck and sure enough the guard is keeping an eye on us.

"You have someone here with you, a lady friend? Or are you traveling alone?" Bridget asks.

"My wife is asleep."

"Where's your ring?" she asks.

"Excuse me?"

"You're not wearing your ring."

"I must have left it in the room."

"My dad says that sometimes men use wedding rings as a lure, whether they're single or not. The wedding ring attracts the woman to the man and they feel challenged to seduce the man," Bridget says. "So, what's in the box?"

"Harmonicas," I say.

"I took you for a bass player. My dad owns a bar in New Jersey. I've seen a lot of bands. You struck me as a bass player— you got a rhythm-section-kind-of-guy thing going on."

"Your father lets you hang out in his bar?"

"There's a restaurant section, family friendly. So, are you somebody?" Bridget says.

"What do you mean?"

"A somebody. You know, someone who is important. You look like someone important."

"I doubt it."

"I see that you have a flask in your pocket," she says, pointing to the cap poking out from my hip pocket.

"Yes Bridget, that is a flask."

"My dad says in the old days both somebodies and drunks carried flasks. For example, Ulysses S. Grant, the Union Civil War general?"

"I know who Grant is," I say.

"Ernest Hemingway. He had a whole collection of flasks. I read *Old Man and the Sea* and saw an A&E special. He blew his head off with a shotgun. Who else? Of course, Hank Williams must have had a flask. So, are you a somebody or a drunk or both?"

"Your dad sure likes to talk."

"Yeah. He says that people don't carry flasks anymore. Now they just carry Xanax."

"All right, now you know what's in the tackle box. What's in the briefcase?"

"My journals. I take notes wherever I go. I collect material."

Bridget's eyes get very narrow. She grabs my chin and pulls it down so our faces are directly in front of each other.

"Okay," she says, "you make up things, so do I. I don't know if you have a woman upstairs or not. But if you do, I have a feeling—you with your black eye and scar—she cares about you so don't screw it up. You're a mess."

"A mess?" I say.

"Wild!" she says, shaking her head back and forth like she's Linda Blair in *The Exorcist*. Then she composes herself and fluffs her hair. She looks at the TV. Zona has wrangled another beauty.

I lean back against the sofa arm and smile. "Bridget, do you know what you want to be when you grow up? I mean, do you have an idea of what you want to do with your life?"

Still staring at the television, she says, "TV—cable, my material is more suited for cable."

Bridget turns and looks at me as if I don't understand. With a quick tilt of her head, ringlet bouncing over one eye, she says, "I'm a comedy."

Country Comfort

He rolls over, slips his finger inside the curtain, peeks out the window. Snow—wet, heavy flakes. Looks like maybe eight inches already. They said it was coming: the big storm. According to the clock on the night stand, it's 6:30 a.m. but she always sets the clock twenty minutes fast. An illusion, an old trick—conjuring time out of thin air, waking up to find twenty minutes that didn't exist before.

Doesn't matter, it's Saturday and no one is going anywhere. Up to thirty inches is forecasted. High winds. Power might go out. This old farm house—spit in the wind and the power goes out.

He turns, looks at her deep in sleep, covers pulled over her nose, chest rising and falling, snoring—a sound on par with the growl of hot rods roaring out at the racetrack, sounds of faraway, hot summer nights. This snoring thing used to drive him crazy, keep him up, wake him, but after all these years this sound brings him comfort. Strange, the little things that bring a man comfort.

Eyes wide open, head racing like it does these early mornings when thoughts are clear, snow or no snow. The farmhouse is cold. He feels it beyond the thick blankets. Frigid air crawls through little cracks, through pipes on the verge of freezing. Mice thunder inside the walls sounding like a herd of buffalo. An entire family is entrenched, huddled in the tufts of pink attic insulation above their bed. The wind blows and the entire house shakes. Another piece of exposed chimney flakes and falls upon hardwood floors. Downstairs the refrigerator makes a weird hum, clicks and clucks. The tick of a clock that never could keep time thumps out an offbeat rhythm. None of this matters lying next to her, next to her body burning like a woodstove. He wants to close his eyes and be where she is, dissolve inside of her. But it's too late. Each little movement causes an explosion in his heart. These are the moments when he is seized, feels some foreign hand reaching into his chest, feels the weight of doubt. These are the moments when he will be discovered trespassing.

He moves to touch her but catches himself. Instead, dress. Jeans, sweater, Smartwool socks, Pac Boots. Descend the back stairwell into the kitchen. One hundred years this house has stood. He and his wife are growing old here—that's what she wanted, to grow old here in this old farmhouse. She's forward thinking. Thermostat turned up, furnace huffs, moans, gulps oil; and the frame, the hardwood floors, the shingles snap in unison: "We heard you. We may be old but we ain't deaf. We'll outlast you."

Brew a pot of coffee, wash wine glasses from last night, stare out the window; the dark kitchen illuminated by morning taking shape. Falling snow creates a dull glow while somewhere, beyond the February sky, the sun rises. Morning dreaming in the country.

Distracted by the "major weather event," a glass slips from his grip, shattering in his left palm as it hits the bottom of the sink. "Goddamn. Whose idea was it to buy goddamn, stemless wine glasses?" Blood mixes with foamy suds. Blood, from his palm, flows like water running from the faucet. He rolls paper towels around his hand, throws the pieces of glass in the trash. He traces the sink with his fingers searching for scattered shards. Remove towels. Little red gashes dot his hand. He applies fresh paper towels to his wound, grabs a jacket, a cup of coffee and steps out onto the front porch.

Snow has accumulated on the bench next to the stacked firewood. The coffee mug melts a perfect circle. The snow falls sideways; swirls, twists in small cyclones. On the ridge, to the east, silhouettes of horses appear between flakes the size of quarters. A familiar pinto trudges down the service trail, pokes his head through gnarly, barbed wire, chews brown vines coiled around the fence. This horse is never spooked. Never moves with the herd. He's watched this horse for years. Blackbirds sweep through tall pines, wings clip branches heavy with clumps of snow; they circle, pick, peck at whatever they can salvage, foraging where they can. Other than the squawking of these dark-winged bandits, Green Valley Road is silent.

This notion of "country" really is silly. He's come to terms with temporary comfort. Even admits to a certain kind of happiness. Still, this nagging feeling of trespassing, of not belonging here, with her—that somehow he is an imposter—persists. He's ill-defined. The more he searches for roots, the more his mind presents him with broken branches and gnarly barbed wire. His hand is just inches away from his chest, so close he can feel the dark crimson heat inside, the muscle pumping an off-beat tick like that old clock that never could keep time. Why doesn't he just surrender, close his eyes and fall into this situation today?

People don't get snowed in for extended periods. Not anymore. Not below the Mason-Dixon Line. Let Mother Nature turn out the lights. Heat water on the woodstove, sip hot chocolate, play dominoes by the dancing fire, get to know one another again. Couples should be snowed in before they get married.

Inside, back up the staircase to the bedroom. His hand has stopped bleeding. She is gone. A gentle moan rises above the sound of running water from the shower. He removes his clothes, climbs into bed and rolls into the depression she's left behind, a spot still warm carved by the shape of her body. He wants to stay there forever.

Acknowledgments

Lightning
Brian Slagle
Skye Sadowski-Malcom
Strange Horse
Hillarie Hough &
the Air Hustlers on the horseshoe at Morgan's
Aga Juchniewicz
Dan Patrell
Holly Smith
Shannon Morgan
Mike Morgan
Elizabeth Cromwell
Adrianna Amari
S. Elliott
Dingo Austin
Gregg Wilhelm
Laura Malkus
(collaborator, anchor, and the dearest of friends)
Doug Oxford,
who taught me about the "deep and the ripple"
Roan

About the Author

Jason Tinney is an award-winning fiction writer, musician, freelance journalist, and actor. His previous books are *Louise Paris and Other Waltzes* (poetry / prose) and *Bluebird* (short stories and poems). Three of his short stories were published in the anthology *Out of Tune*.

Tinney and artist Brian Slagle have collaborated on The Swinging Bridge, a traveling literary and visual arts project, since 2004. He performs with, and is the co-founder of, the award-winning music groups Donegal X-Press (DXP) and The Wayfarers.

As an actor, Tinney has appeared in more than thirty stage productions. He has been a contributor to several magazines, among them, *Baltimore*, *Style*, *Gorilla*, *Her Mind*, *Urbanite*, and *Maryland Life*, which won the International Regional Magazine Association's Award of Merit in the category of Culture Feature for Tinney's article "The March," a first-hand account of life on the front-lines with American Civil War reenactors.

He lives in Maryland.

Skye Sadowski-Malcom

About CityLit Press

CityLit Press's mission is to provide a venue for writers who might otherwise be overlooked by larger publishers due to the literary nature or regional focus of their projects. It is the imprint of nonprofit CityLit Project, Baltimore's literary arts center, founded in 2004.

Baltimore magazine named the press's first book a "Best of Baltimore" and commented: "CityLit Project has blossomed into a local treasure on a variety of fronts—especially its public programming and workshops—and it recently added a publishing imprint to its list of minor miracles."

Thank you to our major supporters: the National Endowment for the Arts, the Maryland State Arts Council, the Baltimore Office of Promotion and The Arts, and various foundations. Information and documentation about the organization is made public at www.guidestar.org. Additional support is provided by individual contributors. Financial support is vital for sustaining the on-going work of the organization. Secure, online donations can by made at our web site, click on "Donate."

CityLit is a member of the Greater Baltimore Cultural Alliance (GBCA), the Maryland Association of Nonprofit Organizations (MANO), Maryland Citizens for the Arts (MCA), and the Writers' Conferences and Centers division of the Association of Writers and Writing Programs (AWP).

Please visit us at **www.citylitproject.org.**